SHINE!

*

*

More Favorites by Chris Grabenstein

The Island of Dr. Libris

THE MR. LEMONCELLO'S LIBRARY SERIES
Escape from Mr. Lemoncello's Library
Mr. Lemoncello's Library Olympics
Mr. Lemoncello's Great Library Race
Mr. Lemoncello's All-Star Breakout Game

THE WELCOME TO WONDERLAND SERIES
Home Sweet Motel
Beach Party Surf Monkey
Sandapalooza Shake-Up
Beach Battle Blowout

THE HAUNTED MYSTERY SERIES
The Crossroads
The Demons' Door
The Zombie Awakening
The Black Heart Crypt

COAUTHORED WITH JAMES PATTERSON
The House of Robots series
The I Funny series
The Jacky Ha-Ha series
The Max Einstein series
Pottymouth and Stoopid
The Treasure Hunters series
Word of Mouse

SHINE!

J.J. & Chris Grabenstein

illustrations by Leslie Mechanic

Random House New York

Text copyright © 2019 by J.J. and Chris Grabenstein
Jacket and interior art copyright © 2019 by Leslie Mechanic

All rights reserved. Published in the United States by Random House Children's Books, a division of Penguin Random House LLC, New York.

Random House and the colophon are registered trademarks of Penguin Random House LLC.

Visit us on the Web! rhcbooks.com

Educators and librarians, for a variety of teaching tools, visit us at RHTeachersLibrarians.com

Library of Congress Cataloging-in-Publication Data
Name: Grabenstein, J. J., author.
Title: Shine! / by J. J. Grabenstein & Chris Grabenstein.
Description: First edition. | New York: Random House, [2019] | Summary: When seventh-grader Piper's father is hired by Chumley Prep, a school where every student seems to be the best at everything, she gets the chance to compete for the prestigious Excelsior Award.
Identifiers: LCCN 2017022751 | ISBN 978-1-5247-1766-7 (hardcover) | ISBN 978-1-5247-1769-8 (hardcover library binding) | ISBN 978-0-593-12392-8 (international) | ISBN 978-1-5247-1768-1 (ebook)
Subjects: | CYAC: Conduct of life—Fiction. | Middle schools—Fiction. | Schools—Fiction. | Contests—Fiction. | Single-parent families—Fiction.
Classification: LCC PZ7.1.G698 Shi 2019 | DDC [Fic]—dc23

Printed in the United States of America
10 9 8 7 6 5 4 3 2 1
First Edition

For two of the brightest stars in our life,
Ronna & Jordan Earnest

*   *

STARRY, STARRY NIGHT

Some people are meant to shine.

Others are better off blending in.

Me?

I'm a blender. But tonight is one of the biggest nights ever for my dad, so I'm here to help.

Dad's singers are onstage at the Municipal Auditorium, waiting for the curtain to rise. I'm off in the wings, dressed in black, trying to disappear.

My dad, Marcus Milly, is a music teacher at Fairview Middle School. His a cappella group has finally, for the first time in recorded history, by some sort of miracle, made it all the way to the biggest show in town: *the finals* of the Winter Sing-Off.

The place is packed. The local news crews are here, too, taping reports for their eleven o'clock broadcasts.

"The finals!" I hear the reporter from Channel 8 say into a camera. "You can't get much closer to the big finish than that!"

Dad's group sailed through the first two rounds with their mash-up of "Let It Snow" and "Winter Wonderland," which, by the way, sounded even better on a stage sparkling with glittery spray-can snow. Now they just have to do one more song for the judges. And they'll do it without instruments or even a piano because that's what "a cappella" means. It's all vocals and *schoop-schoop*s and mouth noises.

I don't go to Fairview. (I'm a seventh grader at Westside.)

That's a good thing.

Music is Dad's life. And even though I'm related to the director, I don't sing well enough to make the Fairview choir. Or *any* choir.

Because I can't carry a tune in a lunch box.

At home, I don't even sing in the shower.

And we definitely don't do carpool karaoke.

Anyway, like I said, Dad has never come this close to winning the big countywide holiday a cappella contest, and I've never been more excited for him.

That's why I volunteered to be his assistant and help out backstage. Dad and his singers are the main attraction. I'm just a moon orbiting their planet.

"This is it, Piper," says Dad, his eyes twinkling with excitement.

"You've got this!" I tell him.

We fist-bump on it.

The curtain will go up for everybody's final songs in seven minutes. I can see other choirs waiting in the wings. Some are in red-and-green outfits. Others in sparkling blue and silver. The backdrop is a row of Christmas trees flanked by a cardboard menorah and a Kwanzaa candle set.

Dad's group is totally focused, doing their vocal warm-ups.

"Ah-oh-oo-oh-ah . . ."

They limber up their lips with a tongue twister.

"Red leather, yellow leather, red leather, yellow leather . . ."

Suddenly I hear a cough!

Dad twirls around. Now there's panic in his eyes.

One dry throat in the soprano section could ruin everything! That's exactly what happened at the Nationals last year. Dad and I watched it on YouTube. A coughing fit took down the top team in the country. (A girl up front was hacking so much during "Let It Go" that she sounded like a high-pitched Chihuahua.)

"Water, Piper," Dad says. From the tremor in his voice, I can tell: he remembers that disaster, too.

"Room-temperature water!" I add, because my scientific

brain knows that room-temperature water is much better for vocal cords than cold or hot.

Cold water could actually hurt a singer's voice—tighten the cords when they need to be loosened. You don't want hot water, either, because it can cause your pharynx to swell slightly. You should also avoid dairy.

I take off, looking for a water dispenser with one of those hot taps for making tea, so I can quickly pour the perfect mix of hot and cold to achieve room temperature. On the far side of the stage, I think I see one.

It's right behind a competing a cappella group.

But they're not doing any last-minute vocal warm-ups.

They're too busy pointing, laughing, and making fun of Dad and his singers!

THE STIFF COMPETITION

"Fairview Middle School shouldn't even be allowed to enter a competition as important as this," I hear one girl say. "They are such amateurs."

She has her hand propped on her hip and is very huffy.

"It's so close to the holidays—perhaps the judges were feeling charitable," says a boy sarcastically. "'Tis the season, and all that."

"Actually, Ainsley," another girl says to the huffy one, "I think Fairview deserves to be in the finals. Their mash-up of 'Let It Snow' and 'Winter Wonderland' was amazing."

"Are you kidding, Brooke? It was more like 'Winter Blunderland'!"

Some of the other kids snicker. Brooke, the girl who

complimented Dad's singers, drops her head a little and slumps her shoulders.

The kids in this group look a lot slicker and more polished than Dad's group. All the girls are wearing the exact same plaid skirt, white blouse, and navy-blue blazer with a fancy crest. The boys are in khaki pants, white shirts, striped ties, and the same blazers.

Dad's choir is in whatever white shirts, black pants, and black shoes everybody could find. Dad, too. His boys are wearing holiday ties. Dad's features a very operatic Santa.

I tilt the twin taps on the water dispenser and check my watch. It's still five minutes to curtain. I have time to eavesdrop.

"We are Chumley Prep," boasts a boy. "We are the best, no matter the endeavor."

"Hear, hear," says another boy.

Chumley Prep is the school over in the part of town where there's a country club with a golf course and where all the homes look like palaces surrounded by gigantic oak trees. Sometimes on Sundays Dad and I drive around over there and gawk at the houses. Tuition to Chumley Prep is superexpensive. That would explain why I don't know anybody who ever went there.

Except, of course, my mother.

Twenty-some years ago, she won a full music scholarship and went to Chumley. My mom was basically the opposite of me. Everything she touched sparkled. From what I've heard, she *never* disappeared into the background. Ever since she was little, people called her a musical prodigy. She could sing, play the cello, and even juggle maracas. Seriously. I've seen pictures in her yearbooks. (I'm not sure how useful maraca juggling is—but still!)

"Did you see the shoes the Fairview director is wearing?" Ainsley sneers. "Can someone say 'fashion mistake'? They're not even dress shoes. They're gym shoes! Black gym shoes—with white socks!"

Several of the Chumley singers chortle and snort.

I can't stand hearing this girl making fun of my father on his big night. He's been working to be here since forever. Who cares what kind of shoes and socks he's wearing? I'm really, really proud of him. Mom would be, too.

But she's not here.

More about that later.

I finish filling the water cup. I'm trying to muster up enough courage to give the Chumley Prep a cappella group a piece of my mind.

Fortunately, I don't have to.

Somebody slips out of the shadows to do it for me.

*

*

*

*

MY HERO!

An elderly man in a blue blazer scampers out of the darkness.

He may be old, but he's feisty. Judging from his outfit, I'd say he must also be a Chumley Prep booster or alum. He's dressed just like the kids, only his blazer is kind of baggy, his khaki pants kind of saggy. I think he might be eighty years old.

"Children?" he demands. "Where is Mr. Glass? Where is your director?"

The kids ignore him. They keep chattering about what's wrong with the other finalists.

He stamps his foot down, hard. "I said, where is Mr. Glass?"

Finally he has their attention.

"I sent him to go talk to the judges," says Ainsley. "They're letting Fairview Middle School go on first in the final round, and that, sir, is one hundred percent unacceptable. *We* need to be the first group on that stage so we can set the bar so high no one will ever be able to top it!"

"Hear, hear," says the boy who, if you ask me, says "hear, hear" too much.

The old man narrows his eyes and says what I'm thinking.

"You, my friends, are not the center of this or any other known universe."

Wow. He's quoting Nellie DuMont Frissé, one of my favorite astronomers.

But the group from Chumley Prep isn't as impressed as I am. Several kids roll their eyes when the man isn't looking in their direction.

He takes a small step forward.

"Think hard about who you want to be, children," he tells them. "Think very, very hard."

The group is stunned silent.

For maybe two seconds.

"Who do I want to be?" says Ainsley. "How about a winner?"

Other members jump in and pile on.

"I want to be famous!"

"I want to be a person who goes to Yale and sings with the Whiffenpoofs!"

The old man shakes his head and walks away.

Me?

I race across the stage with my cup of room-temperature water. I need to make sure all of Dad's singers are at their absolute best.

Because I've never wanted them to win a competition so much in my whole, entire life!

DAD'S RISING STAR

My new favorite song of all time?

"A Merry Holiday Medley"—snippets from thirty different holiday songs in four minutes (everything from "Santa Claus Is Coming to Town" to "Rocking Around the Christmas Tree" to "Kwanzaa Celebration" to "The Dreidel Song") all done Pentatonix-style by twenty middle school kids.

That's what Dad's a cappella group did to win (for the first time ever) the Winter Sing-Off!

Woo-hoo!

They call the group onstage to take a bow. The judges give Dad a trophy. His singers present him with a dozen roses wrapped in green tissue paper and a bright red bow.

"Yay, Dad!" I shout from the wings.

He looks so happy. I swear he's not seeing the Municipal Auditorium when he looks out at the crowd. In his mind, he's on a Broadway stage, just like he's always dreamed about. I clap till my hands hurt. Because I know Dad gave up that dream for me. He wanted to write musicals and conduct Broadway orchestras. But that's a risky career with no guarantees. You need a ton of talent and lots of lucky breaks. Dad definitely has the talent. The lucky breaks? Not so much.

After Mom died, he had to find a steady job so he could take care of me. Winning the a cappella competition? For him, that's even better than taking a bow on Broadway. Well, that's what he tells me on the ride home, anyway.

The next night, we host a big party at our house to celebrate. All the a cappella kids are there, making up funny schoop-schoop songs about the punch. (They do an amazing four-part harmony on *"Sherbet and ginger ale, don't add any kale, ba-doop-ba-doo-ba-dooo!"*)

Teachers from Fairview and the principal drop by to toast Dad with eggnog and iced sugar cookies. A bunch of my friends from school and our neighbors come over, too. Did I mention there are sugar cookies?

"Your dad is, like, officially the best choir director in America!" says Hannah Schnell, who goes to Westside with me. "Too bad this wasn't the state competition." She bites the head off a sparkly red reindeer.

Sometimes in big crowds, I need a break. It's a "blender" thing. So while everybody pats each other on the back, I drift off to my bedroom to have a word with my mother.

Well, a photo of her, anyway.

She's dressed in a black gown, cradling her cello and laughing with her head tossed back. The picture was taken the night my mother performed at the world-famous Carnegie Hall in New York City. Yes, she was *that* good on the cello.

"Everybody's here to congratulate Dad," I tell her. "They were so awesome last night at the concert. You should've heard them. Maybe you did. Anyway, they were amazing. You would've been so proud!"

Music was something my mom and dad loved almost as much as they loved each other.

So, yeah—sometimes I wish I could sing.

Or hum.

BIG MAMA BEAR

Before long, it's nearly Christmas.

I'm hoping Santa brings me this awesome star projector I saw in a catalog filled with scientific stuff or a book by my hero, Dr. Nellie DuMont Frissé.

Dr. Frissé is an astronomer at the Palomar Observatory in California and the host of my favorite show (on PBS or any other channel): *Star Talk*. She also used to be an astronaut, one of the few female African American ones. How cool is that?

At the end of every show, Dr. Frissé winks at the camera and says, "Shine on, stargazers!"

It's like she's talking directly to me.

Why do I love astronomy so much? I guess it all started

back in the second grade. My class went on a field trip to the planetarium. They projected a sea of stars on the domed ceiling, and we all oohed and aahed as, one by one, the constellations were highlighted and morphed into Greekish-statue versions, making the formations easier to see. Leo, the lion. Gemini, the twins. Perseus, the hero from Greek mythology.

My favorite?

Ursa Major, which is Latin for "the greater (or larger) she-bear." Ursa Major was up there on the ceiling of the planetarium protecting her daughter, a smaller constellation called Ursa Minor ("the smaller she-bear").

When the show was over, my teacher had to drag me out of the planetarium. Literally.

I made Dad take me back every weekend for, like, a year.

My mom died when I was three, so I don't remember much about her. But when I look up at the night sky and see the Big Dipper and connect the dots to complete the Big Mama Bear (that's my own personal translation of "Ursa Major"), it's like my mom is up there, every night, looking out for me.

Even during the day or when the night sky is cloudy and I can't see any stars, I know she's still keeping an eye on Dad and me. Stars are like that. They're always there, whether we can see them or not.

My job? To keep looking out for Dad—like Mom would if she were here.

Speaking of Dad, I plan to give him a special present this year instead of my usual original cast recording of his favorite new Broadway musical: an engraved silver frame with a photo of him and his award-winning a cappella group performing onstage at the competition. (And if you squint, you can kind of see me, dressed in black, holding a cup of room-temperature water in the wings.)

I almost have enough money to buy the picture frame because I have a part-time job, walking a pug for Mrs. Helen Gilbert. She's a widow who lives in the senior citizen apartment complex a quick bike ride away from our house.

But that afternoon, as I'm putting Mister Pugsly into his harness, I get some bad news.

THE DOG DAYS OF DECEMBER

"I'm sorry, Piper," says Mrs. Gilbert. "I can't pay you this week. Mister Pugsly had to go to the vet and I had to buy him some medicine and . . ."

As Mrs. Gilbert explains her situation, I can tell how much the little dog means to her. She cradles him in her arms like a baby. When he licks her face, it makes her laugh. Mrs. Gilbert adopted Mister Pugsly from an animal rescue group when he was seven years old.

She told me he'd been at the shelter for ten months because everyone always wants to adopt puppies instead of older dogs. But Mrs. Gilbert thought she and Mister Pugsly could enjoy their "golden years" together. And she lucked out, because Mister Pugsly is the best!

"He also needs special food. . . ."

"That's okay, Mrs. Gilbert," I tell her. "Today's dog walk is my gift to you! Happy holidays!"

I guess Dad will just have to open an empty box on Christmas morning because I definitely won't have enough money to buy him that engraved picture frame.

I take Mister Pugsly around the block. He looks up at me and sort of smiles and snorts. I think that's how dogs say thanks.

Fifteen minutes later, he poops. When I go to scoop it up, I accidentally drop my phone.

Into the poop.

Ugh.

Happy holidays to me.

At least I don't have to worry about the camera lens being smeared. My phone is such an antique, the camera hasn't worked for years.

While I'm cleaning poop off my phone with a plastic bag, Mister Pugsly snorts and yanks, and I get tangled up in his leash and somehow step in the poop that I still haven't scooped. I'm not exactly sure how *that* happened. Maybe the chaos theory of cosmology could explain it. They sometimes call it the butterfly effect because some systems are so complex (like the weather or dog poop scooping) that very small changes can make a huge difference over time. For instance, if a butterfly flaps its wings, it might create just enough wind to throw off a computer's long-range weather predictions. If a pug snorts a funny backward snuffle, it might startle you enough to accidentally step in its poop.

I try to clean the gunk out of my sneaker treads with the pointy tip of a stick. But you can never scrape it all out, know what I mean?

So I go home without any money.

And stinky sneakers.

Since I can't afford to buy Dad that engraved picture frame until Mrs. Gilbert can afford to pay me, I decide to give him a handmade IOU.

This is why, on the afternoon of Christmas Eve, my bed is littered with all sorts of craft project supplies: felt, glitter, glue, scissors, hole punch, sequins, and stars. Lots and lots of stars.

Not to brag, but the finished project is pretty spectacular.

I'm tying a bow around the envelope (made out of felt) when Dad bursts into my room. He's waving his phone up and down excitedly.

"This is the best Christmas ever!" he announces.

I grin because I figure he peeked through the door and saw me working on my awesome craft project.

I, of course, am wrong.

✱

✱

HOLIDAY SURPRISES!

"You won't believe who just called!" says Dad.

I shrug. "Santa Claus?"

"Better. Dr. Osgood Throckmorton."

"Who?" *And how, on Christmas Eve, could he possibly be better than Santa?*

"Dr. Throckmorton is the middle school headmaster at Chumley Prep."

Ugh. Chumley. The kids with the blue blazers and bad attitudes.

"Really?" I say. "Is he demanding an a cappella rematch?"

Dad laughs. "Nope. But apparently Chumley Prep isn't big on losing."

"Yeah," I say, remembering my backstage encounter. I

don't think those kids ever thought they'd lose anything to anybody.

"So many parents called to complain, the music director decided to quit. I guess he was going to retire in June anyway, but he told Dr. Throckmorton the parents might be happier if he sped up his plans."

"So why did Dr. Throckmorton call *you*? Is he blaming you for the other guy quitting?"

Dad chuckles. "No. He wants me to take Mr. Glass's place!"

"Huh?"

"Dr. Throckmorton offered me a job as Chumley Prep's new middle school choirmaster and music instructor!"

"But you already have a job."

"I know," says Dad. "And I love it. But, Piper, this'll be better. For both of us. And when I told him that my wife was the late Antoinette Poliesei, well—that sealed it. She's still something of a legend at Chumley, you know."

Yes, I want to say, *of course I do. You talk about it all the time.*

But I just nod and smile.

"Dr. Throckmorton said there's a plaque with Mom's name on it in the music building."

"Mom has a plaque?"

"Yep."

"They have a music building?" (My middle school has a band room, not a whole building for music.)

"Honey, they have everything!"

"Wow," I say, because it's what I always say when I really don't know *what* to say. "Wow."

"I know," says Dad. "They want me to take over when the winter term starts on January second."

Youch. Dad sounds excited. Me? I'm wondering if he should really be so eager to work at a school where the angry parents of the a cappella kids hounded the old music director into an early retirement.

But I don't want to rain on his parade (especially since he used to be a drum major in college, and parades are sort of his thing). He marches around the room, excitedly telling me more good stuff.

His salary will be doubled.

He'll work with some supertalented singers.

"And I'll have my own music room," he says. Then he adds, almost whispering because it sounds too good to be true, "With a Steinway grand." (He says "Steinway grand" the way other people might say "diamond-encrusted tiara.")

"And since my class load won't be nearly as heavy as it was at Fairview, I'll actually have time to write my own music! Piper, I can work on *Dream Time* again."

Dream Time is the Broadway show Dad's been tinkering with (on weekends and holidays) my whole life. Have you ever had a song stuck in your head for twelve years? Yeah. It's like that.

Then Dad drops the bomb.

"They're giving you free tuition, Piper! You start the same day I do."

Wait, what?

Rewind.

I have to go to Chumley, too?

What'd I ever do to deserve that?

All that really comes out is a swallowed "Huh?" while my mind flashes through a rapid-fire series of images: Hannah and my friends at Westside waving goodbye; a swarm of navy-blue blazers and plaid skirts; Ainsley, that mean girl from Chumley, making fun of my shoes and the dog poop that's probably still stuck in the soles.

"You're going to Chumley Prep, just like Mom did!" says Dad. "For free! Do you know how much an education like that costs these days?"

I shake my head.

"Forty-five thousand dollars a year!"

"Wow."

"I know!"

He sits down on the edge of my bed and shakes his head in disbelief. He's kind of choked up.

"I've always hoped I could, somehow, some way, give you the kind of education you deserve, Piper. And now, well, I can! Sure, I'll miss the kids at Fairview. And my faculty friends. And my dinky little music room with that beat-up old upright piano. But did I mention the Steinway?"

I nod.

"I know you'll miss your friends, too," Dad continues. "But an opportunity like this doesn't come along every day."

"Just on Christmas Eve," I say.

"Exactly! Merry Christmas, honey! And a very happy New Year—for both of us!"

He's so excited, he has to call a bunch of friends and tell them how this has turned out to be the best Christmas ever.

Me? I'm kind of mad. At Dad, for not even asking my opinion before yanking me out of Westside and hauling me off to Chumley. At myself, for not speaking up and letting him know how upset I am. I also wasted a ton of time making a stupid IOU with sequins and sparkles.

I tuck my homemade gift card under a pillow.

Dad won't be interested in a fancy picture frame, not after Dr. Throckmorton Claus has already given him what he considers the greatest Christmas present since gold, frankincense, and myrrh.

Chumley Prep?

Bah! Humbug!

✶

✶

POST-HOLIDAY SHOPPING

Guess what Santa brought me?

One of the Nellie DuMont Frissé books I wanted, which is cool. But mostly Chumley Prep uniforms, a Chumley pencil case, and a Chumley water bottle. Well, computer printouts of them, anyway. Dad did some serious online shopping on Christmas Eve.

The day after Christmas, Hannah comes over. We still have some sugar cookies in a round tin, which Hannah immediately pries open. This time, she bites off the bottom of a snowman.

"Seriously?" she says when I tell her my news. Her mouth is full of sparkly cookie crumbs. "Chumley Prep? You?"

"Yeah. My dad's going to be their middle school music teacher and choir director."

"Piper? You're making a huge mistake."

"Huh?"

"Your father can't do this to you!"

"Well, it wasn't up to me," I tell her.

"Those kids are like alien freaks, Piper. They're *so* not like us. Do you know what kids at Chumley Prep do on their winter break?"

"Not really."

"Well, they don't sit around reading stargazer books and eating Christmas cookies. They fly someplace exotic. On their parents' private jet. Sometimes the jets have a gourmet chef, too!"

"Their jets have kitchens?"

"Yep. Some even have showers! I've seen them on TV. Come on." She grabs me by the hand.

"Um, where are we going?"

"To my house. You need help. My mother will drive us over to the Winterset Collection."

"Why Winterset? Why not Twelve Mile Mall? It's closer."

Hannah sighs. "Because, Piper, Twelve Mile is a *mall*. Winterset is a *collection*. That means it's fancier than a mall. More expensive, too."

"I can't afford—"

"We're not going to buy anything, silly. We're going to observe Chumley kids in their natural habitat."

"Aren't they all gone? I thought they flew someplace exotic for the holidays."

"Not all of them, Piper. Some of them have to stay here and shop, or else the Winterset Collection would go out of business. You need to see what you're up against if your father makes you go through with this Chumley thing."

"Oh. Okay."

Mrs. Schnell drives us to the "elegant and upscale" (that's what they say in all their ads) Winterset Collection. If you ask me, it's just a mall but with shinier doorknobs, marblier floors, fancier stores, and a real piano player instead of prerecorded Muzak.

We do see some kids our own age, including one or two I recognize from the Chumley Prep a cappella group. They're loaded down with shopping bags from Cole Haan, J.Crew, Giorgio Armani, Neiman Marcus, and Salvatore Ferragamo.

I have no idea who any of these people are.

"They're not people," Hannah tells me. "They're brands, Piper. Luxury brands. To survive at Chumley, you need to have the right tags on your clothes."

"Actually, they have to wear uniforms."

"Which you also have to accessorize. Purses, shoes,

jewelry. That's where the rich kids make their fashion statements."

I'm thinking about Dad wearing black sneakers with white socks.

Hannah's right. He and I will never fit in at Chumley.

She drags me to a bookstore, where we flip through some glossy magazines, including one called *The Gilded Tween Scene*.

"See?" says Hannah.

She points at an article about "Today's Hottest, Hippest Hobbies." Apparently, for fun, kids like the ones at Chumley enjoy trapeze arts, yacht sailing, Formula One go-kart racing, summering in the winter, horseback riding, and fashion accessorizing.

Um, yeah.

My favorite activities, on the other hand, are sitting around in the dark and looking up at the sky. I'm sure I'll make a ton of friends when they hear about that.

"Plus," says Hannah, "they all have private tutors and go to academic summer camps. You know I love you, Piper, but you are *so* not in the same league."

"Hannah?" I say, feeling kind of queasy. "Can we text your mother? Have her come pick us up?"

"But we haven't hit half the shops."

"I know. But I can't afford to buy anything here. And I need to walk Mrs. Gilbert's dog. And—"

Hannah grabs my arm. Her face looks like an OMG emoji. She starts hopping up and down. "Look!"

She points to the floor in front of a jewelry store.

There's a thick wad of cash clasped inside a sleek silver money clip sitting right there.

"Come on, Piper!" says Hannah. "This is our lucky day. We're going on a free shopping spree!"

ALL ABOUT THE BENJAMINS

"We can't take that," I tell Hannah.

"Yes we can!"

"No. We can't."

"Haven't you ever heard of 'finders keepers'?"

My friend Hannah is famous for being sort of wild. One time, on a dare (not from me), she drank a whole bottle of maple syrup. It was one of those tiny ones they give you at the Pancake House, but still.

Anyway, I'm pretty sure she *will* grab that wad of money off the floor and stuff it into her purse unless I beat her to it. Which I do.

I glance at the folded-over cash. It's mostly hundred-dollar bills (I recognize Benjamin Franklin's face). And there's lots of them. Maybe ten. That's one thousand dollars!

"You know we can't keep this, right?" I say.

"Yeah, but we *should*," says Hannah. "You could use your half to buy Chumley school supplies. You know: designer handbags. Shoes. Those big sunglasses that look like bug eyes. They have all sorts of discount designer items at the outlet stores."

"We need to give the money back, Hannah."

"To who? It was on the floor. There's nobody's name on it."

"We can take it to mall security. . . ."

"This isn't a mall! It's a collection!"

"Whatever. I'm sure they have a security office."

They do. And we find it. Of course, we pass a lot of interesting shops along the way, and Hannah keeps saying stuff like, "Oh, look. A Gucci bag. You're going to need one of those if you go to Chumley."

Turns out, somebody has already asked the security office to keep an eye out for his money clip. (Good thing it's engraved with initials. It'll make it harder for the wrong person to claim it.)

"Thanks," the officer says. "Not everyone would do what you two just did."

Hannah glares at me. I guess she thinks the guard is confirming her whole "finders keepers" philosophy.

Finally her mom picks us up.

31

It's a very quiet ride home.

"Thanks for taking us to the mall," I tell Mrs. Schnell when we pull into my driveway.

Hannah rolls her eyes because I forgot to say "collection" again.

"Good luck at your new school," says Mrs. Schnell as I climb out of the car.

I smile and wave goodbye.

Then I head into the garage to grab my bike so I can ride over to Mrs. Gilbert's.

"I'm scared," I tell Mister Pugsly while we're out on our walk. He's a very good listener—unless there's an interesting garbage bag to sniff. "Dad just doesn't get it. I won't fit in. I wonder how Mom felt at Chumley. Her family didn't have a lot of money. But she was a star there. I've seen her yearbooks. She was also really pretty, Mister Pugsly. Really, *really* pretty . . ."

(That's something else we don't have in common. I mean, I'm okay. But my mom? She was beautiful.)

We finish our walk. I take Mister Pugsly back home and Mrs. Gilbert pays me.

It's an Abe. Five dollars.

It's a start.

Nineteen more walks, and I'll actually have a Benjamin.

But I'm not sure even one of those will help me at Chumley.

WELCOME TO CHUMLEY.
CAN I GO HOME NOW?

January 2 comes faster than any second day in any new year since they first invented calendars.

I spent the rest of the week between Christmas and New Year's saying goodbye to all my friends at Westside.

"You'll do great at Chumley," said my friend Elyssa.

"You're supersmart," said Charlotte.

"Just don't try out for the choir," said Joe. "Or the school musical. Or band. You should probably avoid band, too."

I put on a brave face. Inside? I'm terrified.

I'm also still a little mad at Dad. Chumley might be his big dream for both of us. For me, it's more like a nightmare.

Anyway, for the first time ever, we're actually driving to school together.

"This is fun," he says. "You and me commuting together. We should get matching Chumley travel mugs. They sell them at the gift shop."

"Okay," I mumble. Dad is so into this, he doesn't even notice how scared I am.

"And guess what, kiddo? I have my own parking space. Actually, it's my spot but it still has 'Mr. Glass' painted on the curb. They've promised me they'll stencil in 'Mr. Milly' later this week."

We pass the mansions with the oak trees and the golf course. Pulling off the main road, we glide through a tall wall of neatly trimmed evergreens, then crunch our way up a pebbled driveway.

Chumley Prep looks like a college campus.

At my old school, we had crossing guards. At Chumley, they have professional security guards who wear earpieces and look like they just retired from the secret service. Guess they'll be the ones who stop me if I try to escape.

Dad pulls into "Mr. Glass's" parking spot. Our Subaru seems out of place next to all the hulking SUVs and Mercedes and Tesla electric vehicles cruising up the main drive.

"Welcome to the first day of the rest of our lives, kiddo," Dad announces as we climb out of our car. He's humming a tune, one from the score of his musical. I don't think I've ever seen him this happy about anything, so I try to go with it.

"It looks amazing," I say.

"It *is* amazing, Piper!"

As we make our way to the main entrance, I see adults who remind me of Hollywood movie stars and fashion magazine models. They all look stylish. And fit. Glossy and glowy.

The kids, of course, are all in uniforms. The parents sort of are, too. A lot of moms wear puffy ski parkas and shiny leather pants. Some are in yoga outfits. Their purses have somebody's initials stamped all over them, just like the ones I saw at the Winterset Collection.

Other moms and dads are dressed in power suits and shoes that glisten.

I also see what looks like an army of nannies toting backpacks.

"Good luck, Piper," Dad says as he puts both his hands on my shoulders and looks at me with smiling eyes. "And, honey, no matter what happens today, remember one thing."

"We have our own reserved parking space?"

Dad laughs. "Okay, there's that."

"You also have a *Steinway grand.*" (I say "Steinway grand" the awestruck way he says it.)

"True. But more importantly, Piper, know that I love you. Always have. Always will. You want me to walk you in?"

"Dad? I'm in the seventh grade. I'll be fine."

"Good luck, kiddo!"

He gives me a quick kiss on the forehead and peels off to the Performing Arts Center.

I take a deep breath and start climbing the steep steps to the main building.

One good thing about school uniforms? Everybody more or less looks the same. It's very easy to disappear into the plaid-skirt background.

CRUSHED

I'm halfway up the steps when I hear a mom down at the bottom of the staircase shout, "Crush it, Ainsley!"

I look over my shoulder.

It's the snooty girl from the Chumley a cappella group.

"Every day in every way, Mom," roars Ainsley as she charges up the marble steps two at a time. She's carrying a ginormous hard-shell cello case. She almost bangs me with it when she powers by.

(I wonder if my mother ever did that with her cello case when she went to Chumley?)

I head to the front office to pick up my class schedule, which is what the "Welcome to Chumley" email they sent to Dad told me to do. I'm carrying a printout of that email in my hands, just in case they need proof that I actually belong at this school.

Inside the building, it's a whole new world. The walls are paneled with dark wood instead of cinder blocks. The ceilings are high and arched—without any foamy pop-out panels. The school office reminds me of a dentist's office, with padded pastel furniture and one of those gurgling indoor fountains.

"Welcome, Miss Milly," says the school secretary.

She hands me a sheet of paper with my class schedule printed on it and smiles at me. I'm suddenly very aware of the collar on my white shirt. It's frayed. Dad couldn't afford to buy everything new.

"You're in Mrs. Zamick's homeroom. That's down the hall. Room one twelve. Don't be late. Mrs. Zamick doesn't tolerate tardiness."

"Yes, ma'am," I say. "Thank you."

On my way to Mrs. Zamick's, I pass through what has to be the Chumley Prep Hall of Fame. There are trophy cases, framed photos, and, yes, plaques.

I can't resist. I start scanning them until one stops me in my tracks.

It's for Mom. Guess she has two—one over in the Performing Arts Center, one here on the Wall of Honor.

It's just her name and the year she graduated etched into a brass rectangle glued to a dark slab of wood. Below her name is a quote from Maya Angelou: "I believe that every person is born with talent."

What if Maya Angelou is wrong? I think. After all, she never met me.

A bell rings. I hurry along to Mrs. Zamick's class.

She scowls at me (and I'm not even late) as I enter the room at the tail end of a clump of shuffling kids.

"You must be Piper Milly," she says, glancing at an official-looking canary-yellow form.

"Yes, ma'am."

"Antoinette Poliesei was your mother?"

I just nod.

Because Mrs. Zamick is giving me a pretty scary look.

"Well then," she says, "I imagine we should expect great things from you, Miss Milly. Great things indeed. I was in Antoinette's class here at Chumley. She made quite a name for herself during her time here. Your mother was . . . very gifted."

I smile sheepishly. Mrs. Zamick is still giving me that look.

"Please find a seat. And, Miss Milly?"

"Yes?"

"Good luck here at Chumley."

The way she says it, with just a hint of a sideways smirk? I get the feeling she and Mom weren't besties.

SCIENTIFIC POSSIBILITIES

My first real class of my first day is science with Ms. Oliverio.

She's not scary like Mrs. Zamick. She's young and perky, with dark hair and deep brown eyes—the kind you'd see in a Disney movie. When she smiles, she doesn't smirk or sneer.

"Happy New Year, everybody," she says after the second bell. "So, have you guys already forgotten everything you learned last term?"

"Not me," says a boy who's seated next to me. He has thick black hair and even thicker black glasses. "My parents gave me a bunch of science books over the break. Plus a Snap Circuits kit."

"Good for you, Siraj."

The kid turns to me. "I'm Siraj Shah," he whispers.

"Piper Milly. I'm new."

"So I deduced."

"How about the rest of you?" Ms. Oliverio asks the classroom. "Still think you remember everything we covered in our last unit?"

Siraj sits up straight, looks around. He's ready for anything the teacher throws at him.

"Well, let's find out," says Ms. Oliverio. "Time for our first pop quiz of the year!"

There are groans and moans from everybody except Siraj. He does a little boo-yah arm pump.

Ms. Oliverio walks around the room handing out sheets of paper.

"Miss Milly?" she says when she comes to my table.

"Yes, ma'am?"

"You weren't with us last term. You can sit this one out if you like."

"That's okay. I'm willing to give it a shot. Science was my favorite subject at my old school."

"Well, I hope it'll be your favorite subject here, too." Ms. Oliverio places the quiz on my desk.

"I like your spunk, Milly," Siraj whispers.

"Thanks."

I take a look at the first question:

1. When upthrust is equal to the weight of an object, it
   A) floats
   B) sinks
   C) moves
   D) stops

Wow, I think. I know this. I glance at the other four questions on the sheet.

Double wow.

I know all of them!

Maybe I won't totally sink at Chumley Prep, at least not in science. Maybe I'll float, which, of course, is the answer to the first pop quiz question.

I turn in my paper before anyone else.

Ms. Oliverio checks my answers.

"Perfect," she says. "Well done, Miss Milly."

"Thank you," I say.

Siraj finishes right after me. He aces the test, too. We smile and give each other knowing nods.

It takes the rest of the class about five more minutes to answer the questions.

"All right, everybody," says Ms. Oliverio after all the papers have been turned in and she's quickly checked them. "Not horrible. You remembered more than I thought. And, Kwame?"

"Yes, Ms. Oliverio?"

"Not only did you ace the quiz, but your bonus answer to question number four was hysterical."

Kwame, a kid with a sly twinkle in his eye, grins. "Well, I know a quark is a subatomic particle, but if you ask me, it also sounds like the noise a subatomic duck might make."

The whole class laughs, including Ms. Oliverio.

"Well done, Kwame."

"I try, Ms. Oliverio," he says. "I try."

"All right, everybody, let's open our books, because science confers power on anyone who takes the trouble to learn it."

Wow! Ms. Oliverio is quoting Carl Sagan, one of my favorite astronomers.

She's definitely a kindred spirit.

At least one hour of my day at Chumley won't be horrible. I figure I can tough it out through the rest of the hours for Dad.

MR. VAN DOOZY

The bell rings.

"Before you go," says Ms. Oliverio, "news flash: the science fair will be held on February fourteenth—Valentine's Day."

"Yes!" says Siraj.

"You all need to start thinking about your exhibits."

"Science jokes!" says Kwame.

Ms. Oliverio laughs. "Ones I haven't heard?"

"Definitely. For instance, last night I was reading a book on helium—"

"And you couldn't put it down," says Ms. Oliverio. "You can do better, Mr. Walker. See you guys tomorrow."

"What's your next class?" Siraj asks when we hit the halls and I look confused.

I check my schedule. "Honors English. With Mr. Van Deusen."

Siraj nods. Slowly. "Mr. Schaack Van Deusen. He's a very interesting character."

"How so?"

"You'll see. Catch you later, Piper."

Siraj shows me where to go.

I head up the corridor, reading every door number along the way, just to make sure I'm moving in the right direction. Finally I find Mr. Van Deusen's room.

I slip in and sit at an empty desk in the back row.

Ainsley, the huffy girl from the a cappella competition (the one who bulldozes innocent bystanders with her cello case), is up near the front, chatting with her posse.

"I quit the a cappella group," I hear her say. "How dare Mr. Glass bail on us like that?"

"I know!" says one of her friends.

"You were his favorite, Ainsley," says another. "His absolute favorite!"

"Yuh-huh," says Ainsley. "And then, to make things worse, Dr. Throckmorton hired that fashion mistake from Fairview to take Mr. Glass's place without even consulting me or my parents?" She shivers. "No thank you."

Great. She's still trash-talking Dad.

She turns around and stares at me hard. "You're his daughter, aren't you?"

"Yeah," I say.

"That explains your shoes."

"Oooh," say her girlfriends.

My face is turning red.

The second bell rings.

Our English teacher does not appear.

"Where, oh where, is Mr. Van Doozy?" says Ainsley sarcastically. "He's such a flake."

A sandy-haired boy who's hunched over and doodling in his notebook says, "No, he's not. Mr. Van Deusen is the best—"

"Oh, shut up, Timothy," says Ainsley. "Nobody asked you. Why don't you do one of your stupid magic tricks and make yourself disappear?"

Timothy freezes for a second. Then he goes back to doodling. I start seriously missing Westside. Sure, we had our share of mean kids, but Ainsley's in a whole different league.

"I have a better idea, Tim," says Kwame, the joker from science class. "Just make that tuna noodle casserole in the dining hall disappear."

Everybody (except Ainsley) laughs. Tim still has his head down, but I can tell he's smiling.

A few minutes later, maybe five, after I've counted six different Shakespeares—three posters on the wall, a bust and an action figure on the desk, a hand puppet pinned to the bulletin board—a bearded man with long, shaggy hair steps into the classroom.

He's about Dad's age and wearing a brown corduroy jacket over a blue work shirt. His tie is an explosion of tiny books. He's fumbling with a paper cup of coffee, a stack of folders, and a bright pink flower.

"My mother gave me this hibiscus for Christmas," he says, putting the potted plant in a sunny spot on his cluttered desk. "What's in a name? That which we call a hibiscus by any other name would smell as sweet."

He sips coffee from his cup and wipes some brown droplets out of his mustache with the sleeve of his sport coat. (Must be why it's brown, too.)

"Welcome back, my boon companions," he announces. "Where's Piper Milly?"

I raise my hand.

"Welcome. Good to have you toiling in our vineyard!"

"Um . . . thanks."

"Okay, pens out. New year, new assignment. Write a descriptive essay about something you did over winter break. Use your senses. Make me feel like I was there with you, instead of at my mother's place in Florida. Now, go! Write!"

I pull out my notebook. Find a pen.

"I'll be back in twenty," Mr. Van Deusen tells us, raising his coffee cup. "Need a refill."

And just like that, he leaves the room. He was only teaching for two minutes.

Everybody else starts writing. Furiously.

Timothy looks up from his notebook and sees me just sitting there.

"Start writing," he whispers. Then he flicks his hand, miming a magic wand. "Piff-piff! Go!"

So I do.

WHO DO YOU WANT TO BE
OR NOT TO BE?

"Piper Milly," sneers Ainsley.

She's finished her essay. Mr. Van Deusen is still out of the room.

"What a stupid name. Piper. I guess it suits you. You definitely look like a bird. Who cuts your hair? The gardener?"

Her girlfriends giggle.

Finally Mr. Van Deusen drifts back into the room, sipping his fresh coffee.

"Okay, my merry band of bards," he says, "who is ready to share their brilliance with the class?"

Ainsley thrusts up her arm, volunteering to go first.

"All right, Ainsley, the floor is yours."

She reads a couple of very vivid paragraphs about the "whiter-than-white, nearly alabaster, snowy, bleached Alps" in Switzerland, where her family went on vacation. (Just like Hannah said they would!)

"Interesting," says Mr. Van Deusen. "But sometimes, we can see more if you write less. Who's next? Sebastian?"

Sebastian's essay is about a cruise his family took. To Mexico. He does a good job of describing the various shades of green his sister turned when she got seasick.

"Excellent," says Mr. Van Deusen. Then, crossing his arms and leaning against his desk, he looks at me.

"Miss Milly?"

"Yes, sir?"

"How about you go next?"

"Well, I . . ."

"Go for it," urges Timothy. He does that magic wand piff-piff thing again.

"Tim's giving you superpowers, Miss Milly," jokes Mr. Van Deusen.

"Use them wisely," adds Kwame. "With great power comes great responsibility."

Nervous, I stand up and read my descriptive essay about walking Mrs. Gilbert's dog, with his "tiny needle teeth" and "smooshed-in snout." I also wrote about the "crinkle of the blue plastic bag" as I scoop up the poop.

When I finish, Ainsley raises her hand.

"Yes?" says Mr. Van Deusen. "You have a comment?"

"Actually, it's more of a question. Doesn't this Mrs. Gilbert have a maid to walk her dog for her? Oh, wait. I get it. Piper Milly is her maid!"

Her friends snicker.

Mr. Van Deusen puts down his coffee. Frowns. Then he takes two steps forward and braces his hands on the edges of Ainsley's desk.

"Is that really who you want to be, Ainsley?"

"Excuse me?" she says, recoiling, like she can smell his coffee breath.

"Is that who you want to be?"

"Huh?"

Mr. Van Deusen shakes his head. "Maybe I read too much Dickens over the holidays. Scrooge, Marley, Tiny Tim." He lets go of Ainsley's desk and starts pacing back and forth at the front of the room. "Got me thinking about character. Legacy. What will I be remembered for when I shuffle off this mortal coil? That Ghost of Christmas Yet to Come always creeps me out. So guess what? I've got a new assignment for you guys. A special project."

"A project?" whines Ainsley.

"Yes, Miss Braden-Hammerschmidt. A project! You know that essay English teachers always make kids write? 'What do you want to be when you grow up?' Well, this is going to be a new spin on that tired old chestnut. A more important, nearly Dickensian question: 'Who do you want to be?' And not when you grow up. Right here, right now. At the end of the winter term, you will turn in your project. To me. I'll be the only one reading your work. So be candid. Dig deep. Think hard about who it is you really want to be in this world."

Mr. Van Deusen sounds like that old man at the a cappella concert. I wonder if they're related.

A boy raises his hand.

"Yes, Parker?"

"How long does it need to be?"

Mr. Van Deusen grins. "Just as long as you need it to be. My suggestion? Keep a journal. Jot down whatever pops into your head. No judgments. No pressure. And then, at the end of the term, tidy it all up into an elevator pitch."

"Huh?"

"Parker, if you and I were on an elevator, riding up from the lobby, you should be able to tell me who you want to be before we hit the fifth floor. Brevity is the soul of wit!"

"But," Ainsley protests, "we need time for *real* homework. We shouldn't waste it on made-up projects based on pointless 'Dear Diary' entries."

"No exceptions. If you don't want to do this assignment, my esteemed colleague, Mrs. Garrett, just told me she has some openings in her English class. They meet this period, too. You can transfer over."

"But this is *Honors* English."

"Your call, Miss Braden-Hammerschmidt. Your call."

I smile. Just a little.

And I already know who I *don't* want to be: Ainsley Braden-Hammerschmidt.

THE GREAT TIMDINI

"Thanks for your support in there," I tell Tim, the kid who was doing the piff-piff magic stuff, when we wind up next to each other in the packed hall between classes.

He drops his eyes and reaches into his blazer to pull out a magic wand. It pops open to become a big bouquet of fake flowers.

"Ta-da! Congratulations on your descriptive essay," he says. "I found it to be very . . . descriptive!"

"Thanks."

"Would you rather have a really, really long silk scarf?" He pulls that out of his ear.

I laugh. "Neat tricks. I'm Piper Milly."

"I know. That's what Mr. Van Deusen called you."

"Right. I was just, you know, introducing myself."

"Ah. Got it." He collapses his magic props and stuffs them back into his blazer pockets.

"So, you're Timothy? Or Tim?"

"Timothy Bartlett," he says with a flourish as he dips into a hand-rolling bow. "Also known as the Great Timdini."

I curtsy. I'm not sure why. Maybe because Tim bowed.

"Mr. Van Deusen is pretty cool," I say.

"No, Piper. He is *extremely* cool."

"What do you think about that assignment? The 'Who do you want to be?' project?"

"I'm already done."

"Impossible."

"I know who I want to be: the Great Timdini, magician extraordinaire. Because Tim is my name and the 'dini' is for *Houdini*. The 1953 movie starring Tony Curtis. Not the miniseries on the History Channel."

"Hi, Tim," says a girl with a wild mop of curly red hair who joins us near the water fountain. She takes a quick drink.

"Hey, Emily," says Tim. "This is Piper Milly. She's new."

"Cool." She shoots out her hand. "Siraj told me about you. You're the science wiz, right?"

"Um, kinda. I guess."

"I'm Emily Bleiberg. So, how about math? Do you like crunching numbers?"

"Definitely," I say. "You can't travel between the planets if you don't know math."

"You also need a rocket ship," says Kwame. He must've cruised up the hall just in time to hear my corny answer. Siraj is with him.

"Hey, Siraj," says Kwame, "ask me where an astronaut parks the spaceship."

Siraj does.

"At a parking meteor," says Kwame. "Thank you. I'm here all week."

"Because there are no holidays this week," says Tim.

"Too true, Timdini," says Kwame. "Too, too true."

"Nice meeting you, Piper," says Emily.

"Ditto," says Siraj. "Although we actually met earlier."

We're all just standing there, smiling, and I realize that Hannah might've been wrong. The kids at Chumley are just kids.

But then Ainsley Braden-Hammerschmidt comes along.

✱

✱

AINSLEY THE PAINSLEY

Ainsley's with her constant three-girl posse.

They're taping up election posters. Apparently, Ainsley is running for seventh-grade class president. Her slogan? "DON'T BE A PAINSLEY, VOTE FOR AINSLEY."

A very tall kid is with her. He's ripping off masking tape with his teeth. I figure he might be an athlete.

"Uh-oh, Carter," Ainsley says to the boy. "Check it. New Nerd Alert."

She points at me.

"That dork cuts her hair with hedge clippers."

Carter laughs. Very loudly.

Ainsley sashays away, saying, "Her father is going to ruin the a cappella group. That's why I quit. . . ."

Her friends follow after her. The way the people who work for a queen do.

"That was fast," says Kwame when they're gone. "Ainsley's got a thing for you already?"

"Yeah."

"Huh. Took her a whole year to hate me."

"Well," I say, "maybe because I'm a dork *and* a nerd . . ."

"Nah," says Kwame. "You and me? We're Hibbleflitts."

Tim giggles.

"What's a Hibbleflitt?" I ask.

"Oh, they're amazing," says Kwame.

"What do they do?"

"All sorts of amazing stuff."

"Can I be a Hibbleflitt, too?" asks Tim.

"Definitely, Timdini," says Kwame, throwing open his arms. "We're all Hibbleflitts!"

"Excellent!" says Siraj.

"Hibbleflitts, unite!" adds Emily, raising a clenched fist.

"Cool," says Kwame. "Now all we need is a secret handshake."

I spend the rest of the day lying low and avoiding Ainsley.

I sneak a look at a text Hannah sent me:

Are the lockers solid gold? Does everybody get fourteen forks in the cafeteria? Don't you wish you'd bought that Gucci bag?

After school, I head over to the Performing Arts Center. Dad tells me he had a good day.

"A couple of kids quit the a cappella group," he says, "but that's to be expected. One girl needs to focus more on her cello lessons."

I nod. And don't let on that I know that girl and what a Painsley she is.

I look around the room while I wait for Dad to pack up his briefcase.

I see the Steinway grand piano, with its lid propped open. Dad's classroom has chalkboards with rows of five horizontal white lines painted across the black. They're staves for dreaming up musical scores. Dad has already filled a few in.

"Come on," Dad says when he's ready to go. "I want to show you something."

We head out the door and down the hall. I know where we're heading: Mom's second plaque. It's attached to a framed photo of Mom posing with her cello that I haven't ever seen before.

"She was just a little older here than you are right now."

"What's the Traub Scholarship?" I ask, reading the inscription.

Dad grins. "It paid for her to study music at the University of Michigan."

"That's where you guys met."

"Yep. I don't know anybody in the Traub family, but

I love 'em all." He rubs my hair. "They gave me the two greatest gifts of my life."

We both stand there and admire Mom's picture and her accomplishments.

Wow.

When we get home, I take Mister Pugsly for a walk.

"Mom's left me some pretty big shoes to fill," I tell him. "And there's no dried poop stuck in the soles, either."

Mister Pugsly gives me a snuffly snort. He *so* understands.

Later, I call Hannah with a quick update on life on the distant planet called Chumley Prep.

"Did anybody offer you a ride on their private jet?" she asks.

"Not yet."

"Well, when they do, don't forget I've always wanted to visit Paris. In the spring."

That makes me laugh.

That night, I make the first entry for my "Who do you want to be?" project. I figure I have all term to work on it so I can do what Mr. Van Deusen suggested: write down whatever, then go back and tighten it up before I turn it in.

WHO DO I WANT TO BE?

My mom, Antoinette Poliesei Milly. Of course, that might be impossible. First, you can't really be your own mother. It's a biology thing. Second, my mother was supertalented and all-around amazing. I am neither of those things. They say you can't miss what you never had. But guess what? I do.

SOME ASSEMBLY REQUIRED

A week later, I'm starting to know my way around.

I feel a little like Nellie DuMont Frissé—soaring in her rocket ship, boldly exploring the vast, unknown voids of a new galaxy. Of course, I'd rather do it with her on PBS or YouTube than in real life.

On Sunday I stream the Nellie DuMont Frissé episode where she answers questions kids have sent in. One of the things I love most is how, even though she's brilliant, she isn't all snooty about it. She'll answer regular questions from regular kids.

" 'Question,' " she says, reading from an email. " 'Do you fart more or less in space?' " She smiles. "More! Because it's impossible to burp when you're weightless. The gas, liquid, and solids in your stomach all mix together. And no, Jimmy, farting won't propel you around the space station like when you let go of a balloon. We've all tried it. The flight suits are too thick. The propulsion gets muffled in all that padding." After a few more questions and answers, she winks at the camera and says her catchphrase: "Shine on, stargazers!"

At school, I sit with the "Hibbleflitts"—Siraj, Emily, Kwame, and Tim—for lunch. Yes, we've proudly embraced the name. Siraj thinks we need an official crest.

"Like one of the houses at Hogwarts!" he says.

Tim brings a new magic trick almost every day. Kwame brings several new jokes. He also makes some funny cracks about Tim's tricks. We all help each other with homework.

And despite what Hannah keeps telling me, no one has flown a private jet to school—with or without a chef on board. Not yet, anyway.

But Ainsley Braden-Hammerschmidt is still telling everybody that Dad is turning the a cappella group into the "ACK-appella" group (she pretends to puke when she says it). Mrs. Zamick is still giving me the stink eye every morning in homeroom.

"There will be no first-period classes this morning," she announces on Monday.

Siraj and I both groan. We *love* first period. That's science with Ms. Oliverio!

"Are you two finished?"

Mrs. Zamick heard us groaning.

"Yes, ma'am," says Siraj.

"When the bell rings, you are to quickly and quietly report to the Hammerschmidt Auditorium for an assembly with Dr. Throckmorton. And in case any of you have forgotten, which I am certain none of you have, elections for seventh-grade class president will be held in all homerooms first thing tomorrow."

The bell rings, and we file out the door.

"What's this about?" I ask Siraj.

"Hard to say. All-school assemblies are extremely rare."

We find our seats in the auditorium, which is pretty incredible—way better than the cafetorium at my old middle school.

Emily is already seated in the row in front of ours. "You guys? In homeroom, Mr. Van Deusen told us this is going to be about some kind of new award!"

I ease into my seat. I can relax. I never win awards, except the ones they give out for perfect attendance.

I see Ainsley sitting smugly in the front row.

Ainsley Braden-Hammerschmidt.

Finally it hits me.

This is the *Hammerschmidt* Auditorium.

Duh.

That's Ainsley's last name! Somebody in her family must've donated a ton of money to Chumley Prep. If she wants to have the school fire Dad, she (or somebody in her extremely wealthy family) can probably do it!

Dad comes in a side entrance with some other teachers. He waves at me. I want to warn him about Ainsley. But instead, I just wave back. Mr. Van Deusen is the last teacher to enter. He has a thick book tucked under his arm and is juggling another cup of coffee and what might be a bagel.

When everybody is finally settled, a balding man with a fringe of white hair comes onstage to stand behind a podium. He must be Dr. Throckmorton. He looks so serious behind his round horn-rimmed glasses. A snowy owl in a tweed suit.

"Good morning, boys and girls," he says with a very proper, almost-British accent.

"Good morning, Dr. Throckmorton," says the whole auditorium.

Except me.

I don't catch on to the call-and-response until it's already hit "ockmorton."

"I have some very exciting news," he continues, sounding anything but excited. "This winter term, we will be conducting a competition for a new middle school award. The Excelsior. This prize will be presented by a representative of the Chumley family on March fifteenth to the student who most fully demonstrates the overall excellence we strive for here at Chumley Prep."

Ainsley shoots up her hand to ask a question.

"Yes, Miss Braden-Hammerschmidt?" says Dr. Throckmorton.

"How exactly do we win?"

"An excellent question."

"Thank you, sir."

"Unfortunately, the Chumley family was not very specific. In fact, they were extremely mysterious about the details. Therefore, my advice: To win the Excelsior, simply *excel*. Remember our motto: 'Be your best, no matter the endeavor!'"

Kwame raises his hand.

"Yes, Mr. Walker?"

"So when does this new competition start?"

"Tomorrow."

"Oh, good. I wasn't really excelling so far today. . . ."

Everyone laughs. Dr. Throckmorton sniffs and pulls out a sheet of paper.

"Here is what the Chumley family has communicated to me thus far about how the contest will work: 'Judges, whose identities will not be disclosed, will be observing your performance for the next several weeks. These undercover judges will decide who wins the Excelsior, which will be awarded at another all-school assembly on March fifteenth. The winner's name shall be enshrined for all time on a plaque in our Chumley Hall of Champions.'"

Now everyone applauds.

I start thinking: if I won the Excelsior Award, I could have a plaque right next to one of Mom's.

The idea makes me laugh a little.

Ha! Like that's ever going to happen.

Unless, of course, "excelsior" means "perfect attendance."

EXCELSIOR!

"Excelsior!" cries Mr. Van Deusen at the start of English class. "It's not just a new prize—it's also a short poem written in 1841 by the great American poet Henry Wadsworth Longfellow."

"What does it mean?" I ask (hoping it really is Latin for "perfect attendance." Or "Hibbleflitt").

" 'Ever upward!' Block the negative, make way for the positive. Aim higher and higher. 'Mine honor is my life; both grow in one; Take honor from me, and my life is done!' "

Everybody just stares at him. I have no idea what he's talking about. Neither does anybody else.

"That's from Shakespeare's *Richard the Second,* which, of course, you will never, ever read, unless you go to college and study English lit, as I hope some of you will do. 'O, let my books be then the eloquence and dumb presages of my speaking breast!' "

Tim giggles. "You said 'breast.' "

"Only because Shakespeare said it first. Moving on. How are you dauntless scribes doing on your special assignment? The *'Quo quid vis fieri?'* project?"

"That's Latin, right?" says Kwame. "Because it sounds like something you'd read on a coin."

"Exactly!" says Mr. Van Deusen.

"*Sit vis vobiscum,* sir."

"And may the Force also be with you, Kwame. Where was I? Ah yes. *'Quo quid vis fieri?'* Whom do you wish to become?"

"I'm finished with my essay," says Tim.

"Already?" says Mr. Van Deusen.

"I'm sorry. That was an accident. I didn't mean to say it out loud. Please forget I did."

"Your wish is my command, O Great Timdini."

One of the girls in the front row raises her hand.

"Yes, Felicity?"

"Where's Ainsley?"

"Ah, parting is such sweet sorrow. She transferred to Mrs. Garrett's class."

"Excelsior!" shouts Tim.

Most of the class laughs. Well, everybody except Felicity.

I don't think much more about the Excelsior Award until I get to math class at the end of the day.

It's all Siraj and Emily want to talk about.

"We can totally win it," says Siraj. "The parameters of the award are wide open. Excellence is the only criterion."

"Agreed," says Emily. "A Hibbleflitt can, finally, beat Carter the jock and Ainsley the princess."

Siraj raises his fist. "Hibbleflitts rule!"

After math, I head over to the Performing Arts Center to see if Dad is ready to go home.

He isn't because he's rehearsing with his new a cappella group.

They sound amazing doing "Lean on Me" with a finger-snapping "doo-wa-doo" intro.

A girl steps forward to belt out the high notes.

"Lean on me . . ."

It's that girl from the Winter Sing-Off. The one who tried to stand up to Ainsley.

"Excellent, Brooke!" Dad says after her big finish. "That was incredible. Kwame? We're glad you signed up. We needed someone to handle the low notes."

"I'm all about the bass, Mr. Milly," says Kwame.

"The rest of you were amazing, too," Dad tells his

students. "We should put 'Lean on Me' into our spring concert."

"Mr. Milly?" says Brooke, raising her hand.

"Yes, Brooke?"

"We usually do a completely classical program for the spring concert."

"Come on, Brooke," says Kwame. "Nobody likes classical music except Mozart's mother."

"I know. But, well—according to my father, anyway—we're expected to learn the classical repertoire here at Chumley."

"Tell you what," says Dad. "We can sing both. Pop hits and classics. We'll shake things up a little. Okay, see you guys on Thursday."

"Oh, Thursday—hey, hey, hey . . . hey," Kwame sings in a rumbling bass line that keeps going lower and lower and lower.

Everybody starts packing up their book bags and heading out the door.

I help Dad gather up sheet music.

"Brooke's voice is pretty fantastic, huh?" he says when everybody else is out of the room.

"Yeah."

"They tell me she also lands all the lead roles in the school musicals."

In other words, Brooke is extremely talented.

Which gives me my second journal entry for Mr. Van Deusen:

WHO DO I WANT TO BE?

Well, if I can't be Mom, maybe I could be Brooke. I don't know her last name. But the way she sings? It makes Dad smile. My singing just makes him cover his ears. You'd think that with two musically gifted parents I wouldn't be so tone-deaf. Maybe I'm adopted. Maybe Brooke is Mom and Dad's real daughter. Maybe we should switch places. Except, then I wouldn't get to walk Mister Pugsly on a regular basis. And I'd really miss him.

✱

BLASTOFF

Things are weird the next morning at school.

Parents in the drop-off lane are giving their kids motivational speeches.

"Winning isn't everything," a dad in a trench coat reminds his son. "It's the only thing!"

It seems strange until I remember that this is Excelsior Blastoff Day. The new contest officially starts this morning. Everyone is fired up and ready to excel, excel, excel.

Except me, of course.

Because there's no way I could ever achieve escape velocity: the speed an object must reach in order to break away from another object's gravitational pull. Even with my own private rocket ship, I could never fly fast enough to pull ahead of all the other stars at Chumley Prep.

"Crush it, Ainsley!" shouts her mother.

"Every day in every way!" Ainsley plows up the steps, looking for someone else to bulldoze with her cello case. She nearly slams into a nanny carrying three book bags.

In the lobby, I see Tim sitting on the floor next to an empty bench. He's sketching something on a pad while the excited crowd swarms around him.

"Hey," I say.

"Hey."

"What are you doodling?"

"It's a new trick I'm working up. All about levitation. My parents bought me a chair suspension kit. You want to come see it?"

"Sure."

"How about this weekend?"

"Great. I'll ask my dad."

Tim nods and gathers up his stuff.

We have trouble walking to our lockers because of the frantic mob slapping up campaign posters on any empty piece of wall they can find.

"Everyone must think winning today's election will help them win the Excelsior Award," observes Tim.

"Vote for me," I hear Ainsley shout, "and maybe Daddy will fly you to Miami with us this weekend on our private jet."

We see Siraj. He seems strangely calm.

"Let this one go, guys," he advises. "Skip politics. We'll play to our strengths: rack up our Excelsior points in academics and, most especially, at the science fair."

"Oh, I'm not interested in the Excelsior," I tell him.

"Me neither," says Tim.

"Excelsior!" screams Carter as he races up the hall tearing down other people's posters so he can hang up more for Ainsley.

"Yo," says Kwame, who's taping up a few signs of his own. "That's called cheating."

"No, Kwame," says Carter. "It's called winning. Excelsior!"

Great. The name of the award has become a battle cry.

In all the confusion, a kid who looks like a kindergartener toddles around the corner.

"I'm lost," she says.

And of course that's when the clanging bell on the wall right next to us starts rattling.

Which scares the little kid so much she starts sobbing.

And we only have five minutes to get to homeroom.

LOST IN SPACE

"I need help!" the little kid blubbers.

Everybody ignores her because they're still busy with their last-minute campaigning.

"We can't just leave her here," I say to Tim. "She'll get trampled."

"What grade are you in?" I ask the girl.

"Kindergarten."

"What are you doing way over here?" says Tim. "That's a whole different building."

"Do you know how to find her classroom?" I ask Tim.

"Kindergarten is over in the Farnsworth Building. It's on the other side of the campus. The *far* side. Across the quad."

I look around. I don't see a single adult.

"Let's go," I say. "What's your name?" I ask the girl.

"Abby," she tells me. "Abby Farah. I'm in Mrs. Sullivan's class."

"Follow me," Tim tells us.

I take Abby's hand and we head up the crowded hall.

As we make our way through the maze of kids, corridors, and staircases, we come across another little kid stranded in a sea of gigantic, frantic eighth graders. He is boohooing loudly, wiping his eyes with his knuckles.

"Are you lost?" I ask.

The boy smiles and nods. "I need help."

"What's your name?

"Victor. I'm in kindergarten."

"Well, come on, Victor," I say, taking his hand, too. "We're headed that way."

We leave the middle school building just as the second class-change bell rings behind us. That means Tim and I are officially late for homeroom and the elections.

We cross the grassy quad (it's like a lawn with sidewalks) and, finally, deliver the kids to their classroom.

"Thank you," says their teacher with a grateful sigh. "Abby and Victor like to go exploring."

"I'm gonna explore space when I grow up," says Abby.

That makes me smile. "Me too," I tell her. "Shine on, stargazer."

She giggles.

Tim and I race back to the middle school building. He and Emily have Mr. Van Deusen for homeroom. They're lucky.

"You're late, Miss Milly," says Mrs. Zamick as I try to quietly slip into my seat.

"I'm sorry," I say. "But—"

She shows me the palm of her hand to cut me off.

"We are not interested in excuses, Miss Milly. Our emphasis this term, as you should be aware, is on excellence."

"But—"

"Do you think people who excel make excuses when they make mistakes? Of course not. You also missed the elections."

"I won!" says Ainsley. "In every seventh-grade homeroom! They already announced it."

She gives me an icy smile filled with glossy teeth.

Like I said earlier, some people, like the Ainsleys of this world, are meant to shine. In fact, even their teeth sparkle.

Me? I'm going to keep on doing my best to blend in.

THE MAGICIAN'S
MAGNIFICENT MANSION

On Saturday morning, I walk Mister Pugsly (he snarls whenever I talk about Ainsley).

That afternoon, Hannah invites me to go shopping with her at the mall.

"The regular one," she says. "Not that ridiculously expensive Winterset Collection."

"I can't," I tell her.

"Why? Is there a Nellie DuMont Frissé marathon on PBS?"

"No. I'm, uh, working on a project at this other kid's house."

"What kind of project?"

"It's all about gravity," I say, because I figure a levitation trick would definitely have something to do with gravity.

Dad drives me over to Tim's house, which is as big as a castle. It's exactly the same kind of house we used to drive around and look at on weekends. It's three stories of towering stone, peaked roofs, and ginormous windows. You could fit our whole house inside Tim's living room.

"Wow," says Dad.

"Yeah."

"Have fun."

Tim's parents are out of town but their live-in housekeeper (a live-in housekeeper!) fixes us some peanut butter and jelly sandwiches—with the crusts trimmed off.

"You want to see my magician's lair?" Tim asks when we're done with lunch.

"You have a lair?"

"It's more like a warehouse. In the garage. That's where the new levitation trick is."

We go through a door off the mudroom and enter his five-car garage, where there are only two cars but tons of props for magic tricks stored in bins and on tall shelves that fill up most of the space.

"This is amazing!" I say.

"My parents bought me all this stuff," Tim tells me. "I've only used half of it. So far, anyway."

"It's like a magic museum," I say, admiring an antique lacquered box with swords sticking out of its sides.

"Mom's just happy I have a hobby," Tim tells me.

"Have your parents ever seen you perform?"

"Mom has. Dad's always too busy. Flying here, flying there, making deals."

Tim shows me a few of his favorite linking-loop and card tricks. He waves his hands and says "piff-piff" a lot. He asks me if I want to stand in the lacquered box while he jabs swords at it.

"No thanks," I say. "Maybe next time."

"Okay, here's the levitation stuff. . . ."

He points to two chairs propping up a board covered in red fabric. He lifts up a small mannequin and lays it faceup on the board.

"I, uh, get a volunteer to lie down on the board like so. Okay. This is the important part. Their center of gravity has to be directly over one of the chairs. This one."

"So there's science in magic?"

"Definitely! There's also magic in science! Especially physics. Piff-piff! Okay, when my volunteer's center of gravity, their belly button, is over the seat of this chair, I put a blanket on top of them . . . pull away this other chair . . . and, ta-da, they levitate."

"Wow!" I say, because the dummy seems to be floating in space.

"Wait," says Tim excitedly. "It gets better. Next, I pull away this board, the one they're lying on, and—"

He stops.

"What's wrong?" I say.

"Did you see the second board?"

"What?"

"The one wrapped in fabric so it looks like a flat red sheet on top of the board I pulled away?"

"No . . ."

"You had to see it."

"I didn't."

Tim starts shaking. "I ruined it. That's the secret. . . ."

"I swear—"

"The hidden board is clamped to the chair," he says, his voice trembling. "I ruined it. The trick's ruined. . . ."

I try to convince Tim that I didn't see the second board.

He just keeps shaking his head and muttering the word "ruined" over and over. I don't know what to do. So I try to get him thinking about something else.

"Hey, is that a swimming pool?" I ask, pointing at a window.

"Yeah," Tim mumbles.

"Can I see it?"

"Fine."

Tim leads me out into the backyard, which kind of looks like a golf course where somebody trimmed every blade of grass with scissors. The swimming pool is covered with a tarp.

"We don't use it in the winter," says Tim.

"Maybe you could turn it into a hockey rink."

"Maybe. I'll ask Dad. The next time he's home."

Poor Tim.

He seems kind of lonely in his big house.

"Hey," I say, "you want to have dinner with me and my dad? It's Saturday night so it'll be hot dogs and baked beans."

"Thanks. But I'm not hungry."

"Dinner's not till later."

"I won't be hungry then, either."

I wonder if I did or said something wrong.

His driver (Tim has one of those, too) takes me home.

Dad and I have our standard Saturday-night dinner and guess what?

Those hot dogs and baked beans taste even better than usual.

FLIPPING THE CALENDAR
AND FLIPPING OUT

January rushes by.

Except for homeroom, I'm doing a pretty good job blending in at Chumley (and avoiding Ainsley). I walk Mister Pugsly every afternoon and twice a day on the weekends. I tell him some of the jokes Kwame tells me.

"You know why dogs run around in circles? Because it's too hard to run in squares."

Mister Pugsly snorts a backward "heh-heh-heh." That's how you laugh when you don't have much of a snout.

I forget about working on my "Who do you want to be?" project. My last entry was: "Not Mrs. Zamick, either."

I don't see Hannah too much. She's busy. I'm busy.

On a snow day, Siraj, Emily, Kwame, Tim, and I go sledding at the country club (their families all belong). I've never been to a country club before. They'll put whipped cream *and* marshmallows in your hot cocoa if that's what you ask for (which I do). And the hills on the golf course are awesome for sledding.

At school, a lot of kids, the ones actively competing for the Excelsior Award, are flipping out, trying to excel at everything at once. Sports, clubs, activities, academics. They're like cosmic dust. They're all over the place.

"The middle school science fair is February fourteenth!" Siraj reminds us one day at lunch, even though I don't really need reminding. I've been thinking about what I might do for the fair ever since that first day, when Ms. Oliverio announced it. "That's less than two weeks away! My heart is beating so fast. . . ."

"Chill," suggests Kwame.

"How can I? The science fair will do more to determine who wins the Excelsior Award than anything else this term!"

Emily arches an eyebrow. "Explain your math."

"There's only one grand prize winner at the science fair. There are three class presidents, one for every grade. There are several players on the basketball team. Many students maintain straight-A averages! Et cetera, et cetera."

Siraj draws a quick ">" in the air with his finger.

"Therefore, the science fair is greater than all other Excelsior endeavors."

He makes a good point. We all nod and go back to eating our food. The dining hall at Chumley Prep is nothing like the cafeteria at my old middle school.

It's an enormous, open room with arches holding up the high ceiling. Lunch is done family-style, with servers bringing big trays loaded down with bowls and plates to the tables. It's awesome. Especially the pasta! We're talking spaghetti and meatballs, baked ziti, or gluten-free vegan lasagna.

"I like lasagna," says Tim. "It's three different kinds of Italian dinners squished together in a layer cake with cheese frosting."

"But that's vegan cheese, Timbo," says Kwame. "The cheese isn't cheese. It's made out of yeast. Yeesh!"

When all our plates are clean, Emily says, "Siraj's logic is solid about the science fair. Winning that would definitely give one an edge in the Excelsior contest."

"Really?" I say.

"Totally," says Emily. "Think about it. The talent show isn't until spring. That takes away Brooke Breckenridge and Ainsley Braden-Hammerschmidt's prime opportunities to shine."

"Mine, too," grouses Kwame.

"Your stand-up routine was hysterical last year," says Siraj.

"Thanks."

"How about you, Tim?" I ask. "Were you in the talent show last year?"

"No," he mumbles, pushing his pasta around with his fork. "But I have a new trick. Piff-piff!"

He holds a water bottle upside down and dramatically removes the cap. Water should gush out. It doesn't.

"Cool," says Kwame. "How'd you do that, man?"

Tim grins. "Very well, don't you think?"

And then he tells us that magicians never reveal their secrets. (Which is probably why he was so upset when he thought he'd accidentally revealed how the levitation trick was done, even though I didn't see it.)

"At least we don't have to worry about Carter Kelso winning the Excelsior," says Emily. "He might be an all-star quarterback, but it's not doing him much good this winter."

"Which, once again, proves my point about the science fair," says Siraj. "This is our big shot, guys. It's like they designed the Excelsior for a Hibbleflitt!"

"Hey," I say, "maybe we should all do one super-fantastic project. We'd be awesome together. Like shooting stars streaking across the night sky!"

"Um, Piper, don't those typically crash and burn?" says Kwame.

"Okay. Bad example . . ."

"I don't want to do the science fair," says Tim.

"But you use physics in your magic tricks," I tell him.

"True. But I hate doing all that data-gathering and hypothesizing. . . ."

Siraj has a very serious look on his face. "As much as I would like to do a Vulcan mind meld with you all, it's probably not our wisest move. Not this year. The Excelsior judges wouldn't be able to determine who did what."

"I guess you're right," I say.

"Game on!" says Emily. "In a competitive but not cutthroat or bloodthirsty way, of course."

We all shake hands and wish each other luck.

Suddenly there's an unbelievably loud metallic crash.

We whip around in our seats.

What we see isn't pretty.

ON TOP OF SPAGHETTI

Apparently, a server just tripped and dumped her entire tray.

The server slipped on the slick mess. She landed on her butt in an orange sea of goop.

Sloppy strands of stringy noodles are everywhere. I can still see a few rolling meatballs.

The server has stray spaghetti in her hair.

Most of the room applauds the tray drop because I believe that's the officially required response in every school cafeteria and dining hall across America.

The poor server stands up. Her white apron is smudged with tomato-sauce sludge. At her feet is a mushy, soggy, squidgy puddle of pasta.

The bell rings. People start standing up. It's time to head back to class.

I count six cloth napkins at our table.

The server needs every single one of them.

I pluck them up.

"What are you doing?" says Siraj.

"She needs help."

"You'll be late to class. The Excelsior judges could be watching."

"I know, but . . ."

"Come on, you guys."

Tim hesitates for a second, but then he shuffles out of the dining hall, too.

I dash over to where the server is wiping off her apron with her hands.

"Here," I say, giving her the stack of napkins.

"Thanks." She starts dabbing herself, cleaning her clothes, face, and hands.

"I'll grab a mop," I say. I see one resting in a rolling bucket.

It's near a table where Ainsley and her royal court are leisurely finishing up their salads. (They must never worry about being late to class.)

"That's Piper Milly," I hear Ainsley say. "She's quite good at cleaning up messes. She'll even scoop your dog's poop."

The girls giggle. I ignore them. I push the mop bucket back to the pasta disaster zone.

"We'll take it from here," says the server, who's with one of the school's janitors.

Behind me, I hear Ainsley and her friends snickering.

I look over my shoulder.

They're all pointing at me.

Because I have a strand of spaghetti stuck to the heel of my shoe. I step on it with my other shoe to pull it off, the way I do when the same thing happens in a bathroom with an overeager roll of toilet paper.

Now I'm kind of hopping and skipping across the dining hall floor.

Ainsley and her gang applaud me. In fact, they give me a standing ovation.

And I didn't even drop anything.

*   *   *
*
*
*

GAME ON

In science class the next morning, Ms. Oliverio reminds us about the details for the upcoming science fair.

I love science fairs. At my old school, I did a project about propulsion using two-liter soda bottles, some pipe, and Nerf-ish foam rockets. The harder you stomped on the plastic bottle, the more thrust you generated, and the farther the foam-tipped rocket flew. Nellie DuMont Frissé would've been proud.

This year, I want to do something even cooler.

"You only have ten more days," Ms. Oliverio reminds us. "And don't forget—I'm looking for something absolutely amazing from each and every one of you."

I glance at the science fair rules, which I tucked into

my binder way back in January. It's the usual stuff about forming a hypothesis, doing research, using math, and following proper experimental procedures. I can do that.

That night, after I take Mister Pugsly for a walk and finish all my homework, I try to narrow down my science project ideas.

I hit on a favorite right away. Nellie DuMont Frissé has a famous quote (I forgot who said it first) that she repeats all the time: "Shoot for the moon. Even if you miss, you'll land among the stars."

I take her advice.

I'll do something about the moon.

I go to YouTube, seeking even more inspiration. Good thing she has her own channel. I've seen (and memorized) most of the videos about the stars and being an astronaut, so I check out one called "The Man in the Moon."

It's fascinating.

Here in America, when we look at the moon, the dark parts form a face. But in Europe, people interpret those darker lunar maria (or seas) and the lighter highlands to be a man carrying a load on his back (like that poor nanny at Chumley every morning). The man is accompanied by a small dog.

Other cultures see the moon rabbit, a sort of sideways floppy-eared critter with its hind legs crossed. One man in the moon that people see is actually a woman with a ponytail, smiling and looking off into space.

It makes me think about how things can look different depending on where or even how you're looking at them. When Hannah and I were looking at the Chumley kids before I actually knew any, I thought they'd all be the same. Snobby. Now I know that some are really nice. It's like I'm seeing the bunny rabbit in the moon instead of the man. I'm looking at the same image but differently.

I wonder if there is some way I can turn the many faces of the moon into a science project.

It's a little after eight o'clock on a brisk, crisp night in

February, so it's already dark and the stars have started coming out to play. We don't live near a big city, so there's very little light pollution.

I can clearly see the Man in the Moon surrounded by all those craters created eons ago by a bombardment of meteoroids. I realize that what makes the moon so spectacularly beautiful from down here on Earth might look ugly, jagged, and scarred up close.

That's when a pretty cool science fair idea hits me.

Just like all those meteoroids that hit the moon!

SHOOTING MARBLES
AT THE MOON

I know from years of planetarium visits that craters on the moon were caused by asteroids and meteoroids crashing into the lunar surface, especially when the moon was very, very young.

For my science project, I'm going to make a model of the moon's surface and perform an experiment to infer how the moon's impact craters were formed.

"Are you going to use a big foam ball?" asks Tim.

It's fourth period. We both have independent study time. We're hanging out in the media center.

"Nope," I say. "I'm going to fill the bottom of an

aquarium with, like, two inches of flour for the moon's inner crust."

"Your fish may not like that."

"Tim, I don't have fish."

"Oh. Good."

"Actually, I could use an aluminum pan. That'd be cheaper. I could make more moons. . . ."

I start sketching my experiment on a sheet of paper.

"Then I'll sprinkle in some cocoa powder. Just a thin layer. That'll be the *outer* crust of the moon."

"And then you bake it?"

"No, Tim. Then I start dropping marbles at varying heights, to show how speed affects the size of the craters. I'll also use different-sized marbles. That'll demonstrate how the mass of the object slamming into the moon could also affect the size and shape of the impact crater. And the cocoa powder? If it works the way I think it will, it'll spray out—just like what happened on the moon."

"You should video it!" says Tim. "In super slo-mo."

"That's a great idea! And on my trifold panels, I could display photos of real moon craters next to photos of the craters I make in my lab to show how similar they look."

"You have a lab?"

"It's like your magician's lair."

"Oh. You mean your garage?"

"Yep. Dad says he'll park in the driveway for the next two weeks."

"That's very considerate of him," says Tim.

"So," I ask, "what are you working on? Any new tricks up your sleeve?"

He opens up his spiral notebook. There's a sketch of a long box with a woman's head and feet sticking out of either end.

"I'm going to saw a lady in half," he says.

"Oh. Did you change your mind about the science fair?"

"No. I'm still skipping that. This will be for the spring talent show."

"Awesome."

"Do you need a lab assistant?" Tim asks. "For your science experiment?"

"Thanks. But I should be able to handle it."

"How about the videoing? My phone has a pretty incredible slo-mo video camera."

And the camera in my phone is broken.

"Thanks! That would actually be awesome!"

"But you have to help me do my magic act when the spring talent show rolls around. Deal?"

"Deal!" I say with a smile.

"Great. I look forward to sawing you in half."

WHO DO I WANT TO BE?

Okay. I've finally figured this out. I want to be Nellie DuMont Frissé. Maybe not the astronaut part. I sometimes get carsick, so I don't think I'd do well in zero gravity. But I want to be someone smart who makes science fun, which makes kids like me want to learn more about it. Nellie's also someone who pushed beyond the limits others tried to place on her. I'd like to do more limit-pushing. With science, anything is possible—even stuff that, once upon a time, everybody said was impossible. Walk on the moon? Impossible, until it wasn't. Be a female astronaut? Not gonna happen, until it did. So, that's who I want to be: Nellie DuMont Frissé!

HAVING A BLAST

In no time at all, after a ton of data-gathering and number-crunching, the big day, February 14, arrives.

Sure, some people call it Valentine's Day. For me and my friends, it's just Science Fair Day. No frilly cards or heart-shaped boxes of chocolates required.

I have all my research written up in cool charts and graphics. I have the side-by-side crater photos. I even have Tim's iPad (he let me borrow it) running a loop of awesome slow-motion clips of marbles hitting the dusty flour—making craters and flinging cocoa spray out in all directions.

I'm also going to set up a fresh flour/cocoa pan and

let science fair–goers drop marbles to make their own craters.

Tim loved that idea. "It's interactive!" he said. "And you can use my marble-shooter robot! My mother picked it up for me when she and my father were on a trip to Japan. It's an alien robot from outer space! People can shoot a high-velocity marble at the cake pan without having to stand on a ladder."

I told Tim I wasn't sure I needed the robot.

He said it would give my exhibit "pizzazz."

I said I still wasn't sure.

Tim looked really sad.

So, yes, I'm adding a marble-shooting robot from outer space to my science project. For pizzazz.

"Good luck, kiddo," says Dad when we hit the parking lot and unload my exhibit. Dad helps me stack my science fair stuff onto a rickety rolling cart. "I'll check out the exhibits as soon as I'm done with my classes."

"We're in the gym."

"Perfect." He takes off for the PAC just as Ainsley Braden-Hammerschmidt's ginormous SUV pulls up.

The driver uses a remote to open the rear hatch and unloads Ainsley's display.

"Do you have your notecards for your speech to the judges?" asks Ainsley's mother.

"Yes, Mother."

"Then crush it!"

"Every day in every way."

The driver lugs Ainsley's science project up the steps for her.

I have to bang our old wheelie cart up the steps, one at a time. I sort of wish Dad had given me a hand. Guess he was eager to go tinkle the ivories on his (gasp) Steinway grand. That nanny who carries more cargo than a pack mule has it worse than me. She's balancing six backpacks while simultaneously tugging a rolling suitcase.

"Do you need help?" I ask.

"Thank you," she says. "But your hands are full."

"Not as full as yours!"

I take three backpacks. I sling one over my shoulders, loop two more over my arms, and still have a free hand to drag my wheelie cart.

I haul my stuff to the gymnasium and find my assigned spot. It's right between Siraj and Ainsley.

"This is it, Piper," says Siraj. "The big day."

"Yeah. Where's Emily?"

"Over there," says Siraj. "We both arrived super early this morning. Neither of us could sleep last night."

I see that his exhibit is all set up and ready to go.

And, as it turns out, we're both playing with marbles.

*

*

BRAINPOWER

Siraj has some sort of slanted triangular array of pegs where you pour marbles in the top and they make their random way down to bins on the bottom—bouncing right or left with every peg they hit.

"It's a quincunx for probability distribution analysis," says Siraj. "Since there is an equal chance of a marble bouncing left or right at each peg, the marble stacks in the bins below will, on average, form the classic bell-shaped curve of normal distribution."

"Fantastic," I say.

I dump a tub of marbles into the top. They do not end up in the "classic" bell-shaped curve Siraj and I were expecting. In fact, a few of them wind up at the far edges of the quincunx's bottom rack.

"That'll happen," says Siraj. "Sometimes."

I give him a quick tour of my crater creation exhibit.

"Awesome," he says after he shoots a marble out of the Japanese robot's belly to blast his own impact crater on the surface of my cake-pan moon.

I glance over at Ainsley's trifold cardboard display. Her exhibit is titled "Gemstones: Earth's Most Expensive Crystallized Minerals." It appears to be a collection of her mother's jewelry and some crystals she grew in a fridge with salt and food coloring.

When Ms. Oliverio and the other science fair judges come up our row of exhibits, Ainsley launches into a speech she reads off pink notecards about diamonds being "the most beautifully compressed carbon atoms imaginable" and rubies being red "because of our red-hot friend chromium."

When it's Siraj's turn, he does a very dry, kind of mumbled recitation of probability formulas. He also sweats a lot.

"Very good, Siraj," says Ms. Oliverio. "Piper?"

It's my turn.

I tell the judges my top-line inferences. "The rounder the object hitting the moon, the faster an object is traveling, the farther away an object is from the moon, the larger the crater it creates."

Then I let them take turns shooting marbles at my lunar-surface cake pan.

Ms. Oliverio loves the robot. "It reminds me of the way Nellie DuMont Frissé makes astronomy fun in her videos. I think she'd be impressed by your project, Piper."

Could there be a higher compliment? No. There could not.

"Tim let me borrow the robot," I tell the judges.

"Because he's an excellent showman," says Ms. Oliverio. "Good job, Piper."

After the judges visit all the exhibits, we have to leave so they can deliberate.

The gym is still locked at three, when classes are over.

Dad's waiting outside the doors. So is an eager and anxious crowd. Siraj has all his fingers crossed. Probably his toes, too. Emily is bobbing up and down on her toes like she has to go to the bathroom.

Ainsley looks like she's ready to sign autographs.

"Have you guys heard anything?" asks Dad.

I shake my head. Siraj does the same. We're both too nervous to speak.

"If the Hibbleflitts want a shot at the Excelsior," says Emily, still bouncing up and down, "one of us has to win this thing!"

Finally someone inside unlocks the doors. We all race to our exhibits.

"Yes!" says Dad with a mighty arm pump.

There's a blue ribbon hanging off my trifold board.

I took first place!

Ainsley's gemstones and Siraj's quincunx both earned an honorable mention. So did Emily's exhibit about the geometry of origami (she called it Origometry)!

Ainsley isn't happy with her yellow ribbon.

"Are you two trying to ruin my life?" she hisses at Dad and me.

Then she stomps out of the gym as Tim comes in.

"How'd we do?" he asks.

I show him the blue ribbon. "First place! Thank you so much, Tim. I couldn't've done this without you!"

"You're welcome. So, now that the science fair is finally over, you want to come to my house this weekend? Mom bought me a new trick."

"She doesn't have time," says Siraj.

Tim looks confused. Me too.

"Piper's in the lead for the Excelsior Award now," says Emily, who's drifted over to join us.

"You guys?" says Dad. "I don't think . . ."

"It's true, Mr. Milly," says Siraj. "This is the only single-winner competition of the entire winter term. Therefore, we have to assume that Piper now has the best shot of beating Ainsley and Carter and all the popular kids who always win everything."

"She needs to focus, sir," Emily tells Dad. She turns to

Tim. "Sorry, Tim. This isn't just about Piper. It's about all of us."

Tim looks at me. His eyes are so sad.

"The new trick is amazing," he says.

"I'm sure it is," I tell him. "But if Siraj is right . . ."

"He is," says Emily. "Please, Piper? Do it for every kid that Ainsley Braden-Hammerschmidt ever called a dork or a nerd."

"Or a dweeb," says Siraj. "She calls me that sometimes, too."

"Tim, you have to understand," says Emily. "Piper needs to find more things to excel at. She won't have time for magic tricks."

Tim looks hurt. "You should always make time for magic."

I know Tim is right. But I'm also remembering what Mr. Van Deusen said about the word "excelsior" meaning "Ever upward!"

"Aim higher and higher," he told us.

Where would Nellie DuMont Frissé be if she and the whole space program didn't aim as high as they possibly could? It's like that song lyric she quoted in one of her videos: "Don't tell me the sky's the limit when there are footprints on the moon."

I have a chance of boldly going where no one like Siraj, Emily, Kwame, Tim, or me has ever gone before.

I need to do this thing. It's time to do what Nellie would do. It's time to push a few limits.

"Don't worry," I tell Tim. "There will be plenty of time for magic. I promise. Right *after* March fifteenth!"

WHO DO I WANT TO BE?

Still not sure, Mr. Van Deusen. But today I feel a little like one of Siraj's marbles, bouncing around and willing to end up wherever fate and gravity and the laws of probability take me—even if it's a slot I never dreamed of landing in. It might be time for me to imagine my own footprints on a distant moon. If not for me, then for all those counting on me. So, okay, today I know exactly who I want to be—the winner of Chumley Prep's first-ever Excelsior Award! The one who gets a plaque right next to Mom's!

*

*

ACHIEVING ORBIT

That evening, there's a science fair reception.

Ms. Oliverio puts dry ice in the punch bowl so it looks mad-scientist-ish. We stand in front of our exhibits while parents we don't know come up and tell us how brilliant we are. It's awesome.

Dad's at the party and people are congratulating him, too.

"You must be so proud of your daughter," says one person after another.

"I am," says Dad. "Always have been."

Ainsley Braden-Hammerschmidt and her family skip the science fair celebration. She is so mad at me. It's like I stole something she thought she was entitled to.

Some parents chatting with Dad find out that not only is he a Chumley Prep music instructor, but he is also the composer of several show tunes that could become a musical.

"I advise some investors in New York City who might be interested in backing a Broadway show," says Brooke's father, Mr. Breckenridge. He flicks Dad his business card. "We should talk."

Dad beams.

It feels fantastic to be a winner.

It feels even better to see Dad so happy.

You know what? I think I'm all done with "blending in."

The next day, starting in homeroom, Ainsley and her friends are whispering, pointing, and shooting me nasty looks whenever and wherever they can.

Between periods, I catch up with Siraj and Emily near the girls' bathroom, which is closed for service.

They want to brainstorm new ways for me to "excel."

"You should consider joining the Mathletes squad with Emily," suggests Siraj.

"We'd love to have you," says Emily.

"So, what does a Mathletes team do?" I ask. "We never had one at Westside."

"We compete in mathematics competitions," says

Emily. "They're formatted like a quiz show on TV. Last year, we came in second at the state championship. However, this year—"

She stops in midsentence because Ainsley is sashaying up the hall—trailed by what looks like half the middle school.

Ainsley doesn't look happy.

"Hello, *Piper Milly.*" Contempt drips off every syllable in my name. "What are you three doing? Shooting marbles at each other's butts?"

The crowd giggles. I'm ready to start blending in again. When you aim for the stars, sometimes you run into angry asteroids named Ainsley.

She prowls forward—like a lioness moving in for the kill. "I certainly hope you enjoyed your little science fair victory party last night. Because this is war."

When Ainsley says that, the whole crowd goes, "Ooooh."

Well, everybody except me and my friends. We just sort of tremble in fear.

BURSTING MY BUBBLE

"War?" says Siraj, because I'm too stunned to say anything myself.

"You heard me, *Siraj*. Your friend may have won a blue ribbon, but that doesn't mean she deserves to win the first-ever Excelsior Award. Why? Let me count the ways. One: Piper Milly is a new student. The Excelsior should go to a loyal Chumley student who has attended this institution for a minimum of seven years."

"I've done that," says Siraj.

Ainsley ignores him and steamrolls ahead. "Two: Piper Milly's winning science project was absurd. Shooting marbles at an unbaked cake? That's just sad. Three, and most importantly: Piper Milly is not, by any stretch of the imagination, a person who excels."

"And how could you possibly know that?" asks Emily.

"Easy. *I* am a person who excels. And when I look in the mirror, I do not see Piper Milly. I don't see you, Emily, or you, either, Siraj. I see me!"

"Ooooh," the crowd says again. I think they're itching for a fight.

"Help!" cries a voice.

It isn't mine, even though that's exactly what I'm thinking inside: *HELP!!!!*

THIS STINKS. LITERALLY.

"Help!" the man cries again from inside the closed-for-service girls' bathroom.

"This toilet won't stop flushing! Help, please!"

Ainsley sneers at me. "Piper, I'm sure that with all your poop-scooping experience, you know how to deal with any and all toilet-related emergencies."

I can hear a toilet flushing over and over again and water sloshing out of a bowl.

Ainsley laughs.

The bell rings.

The crowd disperses. Fast. My friends, too.

"Can't be late for class," Siraj says over his shoulder as he practically trots up the hall. "Big test."

"Yeah," says Emily. "Huge test. Gotta run. But think about Mathletes."

She and Siraj vanish.

"Help!" shouts the man in the bathroom. "Somebody? Anybody?"

I'm alone in the hall.

It's just me, the panicked voice, and the gross, foamy water seeping out from underneath the bathroom door. I take a deep breath, pinch my nose, and step into a disaster zone.

I see a wide-eyed, terrified janitor clutching a plunger.

He's much younger than all the other custodians at Chumley. He's also frozen with panic.

"It's my first day!" He has to shout to be heard over the cascading water.

I go into full Apollo 13 mode. You know—where you have to solve a problem to avert a disaster using only what's on hand, like the three astronauts did during the doomed Apollo 13 mission.

"Did you plunge it?"

"It's not a clog. They're going to fire me. I know they are. . . ."

"Sir?" I say, in my firmest, calmest astronaut voice. It's the way I imagine Nellie DuMont Frissé sounding when people around her start freaking out. "Did you try shutting off the water?"

"What?"

Oh-kay, I think. How come I know more about fixing an overflowing toilet than a professional custodian? Maybe he's a substitute janitor (like a substitute teacher).

Water keeps gurgling over the lip of the bowl. Soggy wads of toilet paper and crumpled hand towels are drifting across the floor like lumpy jellyfish.

I look behind the janitor and see a narrow metal door built into the wall.

There's a sign on it: SHUTOFF VALVE.

"Behind that door!" I shout. "There's a shutoff valve!"

"Are you sure?"

"Yes! Read the sign!"

I can't believe this guy. He must be Dr. Throckmorton's nephew or something. How else did he get this job?

Finally he pops open the cabinet, finds the valve, and—with a mighty twist—rotates it to the off position. The water stops gushing out of the commode.

"It worked. Thank you!"

"You're welcome."

The janitor is thrilled.

Me?

I'm thinking about what Ainsley said and wondering what a person who excels looks like.

And I'm pretty sure they don't have socks and shoes that are soggy and squishy.

*

*

MORE BLACK HOLES

A week later, as I'm hiking up the front steps to school, I realize I haven't seen that nanny toting backpacks for a while.

Maybe she found a better job. One where she doesn't have to be a human luggage cart.

Ever since the science fair, I've been busy—trying to think of new ways to excel (Mathletes? Water polo? Competitive dog walking?). Siraj, Emily, and Kwame are full of suggestions.

"You should try out for the girls' hockey team," said Kwame. "Or the basketball team. Hey, you know why Cinderella was so bad at sports?"

"No," I told him.

"Because her coach was a pumpkin."

I laughed. Then I did try out for the hockey team, because I can skate some. I ended up inside the goal. On my butt.

Emily said I should try out for the chess team.

I did. Turns out, I'm better at checkers.

"The Doodlers Club!" said Siraj. "It's not a very ambitious goal, but any club membership might make you look better to the Excelsior judges."

I attended one meeting and drew an incredibly awesome spaceship cruising through the stars. But I don't think anybody can really excel at doodling. That's why they call it doodling.

I'm going through a mental checklist of other clubs as I reach the top of the stairs. I'm so lost in thought, I almost don't see Tim.

"Hey," I say.

He doesn't say "Hey" back.

"Where's my robot?" he asks.

I'm sort of surprised. "I, uh, didn't bring it with me to school today. . . ."

"Because you don't need it anymore," says Tim.

"I'm sorry, Tim. It's just that—"

"Crush it, Ainsley!" I'm interrupted by Mrs. Braden-Hammerschmidt, down in the drop-off lane.

"Every day in every way!" shouts Ainsley as she charges up the steps with her cello case. "Excelsior!"

She bounds up the stairs, two at a time, and sees me and Tim and the way Tim is kind of glaring at me.

"Oooh. What's this? Trouble in Nerdsylvania?"

"This is none of your business, Ainsley," says Tim. He turns to face me. "The marble shooter is mine and I want it back."

Ainsley giggles and breezes into the building.

"Tim, I'm sorry if—"

"Just bring me my robot. I need it for a magic trick."

"Okay."

He marches off.

There's a commotion at the foot of the steps.

"Where's Dr. Throckmorton?" demands a man standing beside Carter Kelso. Carter's decked out in his Chumley Prep letter jacket—probably to remind everybody what a huge football star he is. "I need to see Dr. Throckmorton."

"Is there a problem, sir?" asks a security guard.

"You bet there is! This school is cheating my son out of what is rightfully his."

"You're Carter's father?"

"That's right. And do you know how much money I donate to this school every year?"

"No, sir."

"Well, I sure do. I need to see Dr. Throckmorton. Immediately."

The guard escorts Mr. Kelso up the steps. "Why don't we go see if he's in his office."

"He'd better be!" fumes Mr. Kelso. "I paid for that office!"

In science, we watch a documentary about Rachel Carson, the conservationist who wrote a book called *Silent Spring*.

"She's one of my heroes," says Ms. Oliverio when the movie's done. "Mr. Van Deusen's, too."

That makes me smile. Rachel Carson is Ms. Oliverio and Mr. Van Deusen's Nellie DuMont Frissé.

"We're both very interested in protecting our environment. So every year, on what we call Rachel Carson Day, we lead a team of Chumley students who volunteer to clean up a mile of highway. Next Monday—"

She is interrupted by Dr. Throckmorton's voice coming out of the ceiling speakers.

"Pardon the interruption," he says. "I have an announcement to make in regard to the ongoing Excelsior Award competition."

This is big. We haven't heard any "official" news about the contest since that first assembly way back in January. Now it's almost the end of February. There are only three weeks left until someone wins the competition.

Siraj shoots me a big thumbs-up. He's still convinced that I'm going to win the Excelsior because I won the science fair.

"It has been brought to my attention," Dr. Throckmorton

continues, "that the Excelsior competition has, thus far, not been fair to all of our students, particularly those who excel at fall and spring sports. Therefore, to level the playing field, so to speak, we will be hosting an all-sports athletic exhibition next Monday. Coach Tucci and Coach Marcus will select the top athletes for football, baseball, volleyball, field hockey, soccer, lacrosse, and softball. Those teams will then engage in a series of short intramural scrimmages next Monday, immediately after school."

The bell rings.

"That is all," says Dr. Throckmorton. "Have a pleasant and productive day."

"We'll talk more about the public service project tomorrow," says Ms. Oliverio as everybody packs up their books to change classes.

"Tough break," Siraj tells me when we're in the hall. "I did not see that coming. Unfortunately, sporting events have champions and clear winners. After next Monday, you may no longer be in the lead for the Excelsior."

WHO DO I WANT TO BE?

Well, Mr. Van Deusen, given the new wrinkle in the Excelsior Award competition, I wouldn't mind being a superstar athlete. But I'd need to become one by next Monday. I've never really played any organized sports. Except soccer.

When I was six. And we weren't very organized. But I did make some good friends—something that keeps getting harder and harder the more I focus on the Excelsior. Tim is upset because I don't have time to even think about magic. I also don't have time to hang with my old friends like Hannah. It makes me wonder: Is there any way to be a person who wins without losing all your friends? Probably not. I wonder if Nellie DuMont Frissé has any friends.

DECISIONS, DECISIONS

The week flies by.

All the athletes are practicing for the intramural games.

Come next Monday, I won't be the only student with a clear-cut victory.

I fear my chance at winning the Excelsior Award might be slipping out of my grip. It's like I'm on a spacewalk and somebody is sawing through the tether connecting me to the mother ship. One more cut and I'll drift off into the vast nothingness surrounding the constellation Loserus Major.

In English on Friday, Mr. Van Deusen gives us *his* pitch for the after-school highway litter removal project.

"I'm like Shakespeare," he says. "I find 'tongues in

trees, books in the running brooks, sermons in stones, and good in everything.'"

Kwame has a squeamish look on his face. "You found a tongue in a tree?"

"It's a metaphor, Kwame. Work with me."

Mr. Van Deusen holds up a clipboard with a sign-up sheet.

It's empty.

"Okay, my merry pranksters, as you know, we have a lot of competition on Monday. Intramural athletics at three. Mathletes are meeting at four-thirty. The Bathletes are probably hosting their bubble bath competition on Monday, too."

We all laugh.

"So if you're not an athlete, a Mathlete, or a Bathlete, we need you!"

Tim raises his hand. "I'll do it," he says.

"Excellent! Who else? We leave at three, we pick up trash for an hour, you're back here by four-thirty. So you could, technically, go to the Mathletes meeting."

I raise my hand. "I'll sign up."

I'm hoping I can do both. The trash pickup because it's a good thing to do (plus I really like Mr. Van Deusen and Ms. Oliverio). And Tim will be there. Our friendship could use a little tidying up, too.

I'll join Emily at the Mathletes meeting because making that team might help my Excelsior chances.

"Anybody else?" asks Mr. Van Deusen.

No hands go up.

"'I burn, I pine, I perish' awaiting your response."

Still nothing. Even though, I think, he was quoting Shakespeare again.

"Okay," he says, "did Ms. Oliverio talk to you guys about Rachel Carson?"

A bunch of us nod.

"Who knows why Ms. Carson gave her book the title *Silent Spring*?"

"Because she had spring allergies and got laryngitis?" cracks Kwame.

"Good guess, Mr. Walker, but, alas, I am afraid you are incorrect. Thanks for playing. No, my faithful friends, she called it *Silent Spring* because she imagined a world so polluted that there weren't any more birds. No merry chirping in the trees. No robins bobbing for worms. 'What, gone without a word?' If we don't clean up and protect our earth, spring may grow as quiet as Juliet's tomb."

Still no volunteers.

Mr. Van Deusen slurp-sips from a paper cup filled with what, at the end of the period, has to be very cold coffee.

"One other thing. Participation in the highway cleanup counts as public service, which always looks good on a college application."

Six more hands shoot up.

"Huzzah!" says Mr. Van Deusen, which, I think, is how Shakespeare would say "Yay!"

TRASH TALK

I spend the weekend walking Mister Pugsly and reaching out to Tim with texts.

I even put a "piff-piff" in one.

He does not respond.

On Monday the whole school is decorated with banners and bunting and pom-poms. Imagine a homecoming football game taking place on the same day as the lacrosse, soccer, baseball, tennis, and cross-country championships. There's even a fourth-period pep rally.

Ainsley Braden-Hammerschmidt is, of course, captain of the girls' lacrosse team. I figure she probably likes whacking people with that net-on-a-stick thing.

I see Tim during our independent study time in the media center.

He pretends he doesn't see me.

At 3 p.m., those of us who signed up for the Rachel Carson Day trash removal project line up to board the bus that will take us to the cleanup site.

I see Siraj.

"Hey!" I say, and give him a wave.

He's with Kwame and Emily.

Tim's there, too.

I muster my courage and try, one more time.

"Hey," I say to Tim.

"Hey," Tim says back.

"Got any new tricks?"

"A few."

"Cool. I've got your robot in my locker. So you can do that trick, too."

"Thank you. I appreciate that."

"I'm sorry I didn't give it back right away."

Tim looks down at his shoes.

"Piper?" he mumbles.

"Yeah?"

"There's really no such thing as a magic trick with a marble-shooting robot."

"Really? Because I was totally looking forward to seeing it."

Tim looks up. I notice a faint smile tugging at his lips. Phew. I think we can be friends again.

The bus drops us off along the side of a pretty busy highway.

The shoulder of the road is ground zero for a meteor shower of bottles, cans, tires, hubcaps, French fry holders, and discarded shopping bags. And shoes. Somebody tossed out a pair of high heels.

Cars and eighteen-wheelers zoom past. Some toss out crushed fast-food bags and half-filled drink cups just to give us a little more litter to pick up. We're decked out in bright orange vests with even brighter reflective strips.

A lot of the garbage is gross. And slimy. I am sooooo glad Ms. Oliverio thought to pack a box of rubber gloves.

"How long do we have to do this for it to count?" whines a girl named Gabrielle.

"I need you guys to spend at least an hour out here," says Ms. Oliverio.

"Fine." Gabrielle activates the timer on her phone. "That's, like, fifty minutes from now."

"We'll have to leave then, too," Emily reminds me. "The Mathletes meeting is at four-thirty."

I drag my big plastic bag over to where Tim is plucking trash.

"Want to share?" I ask, opening up the bag.

"Sure."

We toss trash into the black sack.

All of a sudden, I hear something cooing.

"Is that a bird?" I say, looking around.

"Yes," says Tim. "I think it's coming from your bag, Piper."

"No way," I tell him. "We put everything in this bag. We did *not* drop a bird inside it."

Tim puts his ear to the bag. I hear more cooing. "Sure sounds like we did."

Siraj, Kwame, and Emily come over.

"Um, Tim?" says Kwame. "Why are you listening to a trash bag?"

"Shhh!" says Tim. "I think it might be . . ."

He takes a dramatic pause.

"A-liiiiiive!"

He reaches into the bag and pulls out a rainbow-colored toy bird. It flaps its wings and takes flight.

The rest of us laugh.

"See?" says Tim. "I told you. There's always time for magic. By the way—no birds were hurt in the performance of that trick."

"But I heard the bird," I say.

"Because I've been studying ventriloquism."

"Wow! Cool."

We keep picking up trash and stuffing it into bulging

black bags. When we hit the half-mile mark, I hear Gabrielle's phone blare what sounds like a fire alarm.

"That's an hour!" she proclaims.

She taps an app on her phone. Pretty soon other kids start doing the same thing. Five minutes later, all sorts of black town cars and SUVs are pulling over on the side of the road. Everybody called an Uber or their family driver.

"Come on, Piper," says Emily, waiting for me at her car. "The Mathletes meeting is in fifteen minutes. You need to be there."

"If you merry minstrels want to knock off, you can," says Mr. Van Deusen. "You put in your hour. It counts. You've done your duty. You may go in peace."

I turn around and look back at the half mile we cleaned up.

"But it looks so much better behind us," I say.

"True," says Kwame.

"So let's keep going. Emily? Mathletes is your thing. You don't need me."

"But *you* need Mathletes. For the Excelsior!"

"I guess. But right now, I think this highway needs me more."

"You're sure?"

"Positive."

"Okay. See you guys tomorrow." Emily climbs into her car and heads back to school.

Me? I head back to the trash.

COURSE CORRECTIONS

"Hey, Tim?" says Kwame. "You know any magic tricks to make garbage disappear? Can't you just wave a wand or something?"

"Sorry," says Tim. "I left my wand at home. . . ."

We all start picking up litter again.

As I'm grabbing soggy junk out of the weeds, I come up with an idea.

"Okay, guys," I say. "Whoever picks up the most trash in the next fifteen minutes doesn't have to do any work for the fifteen minutes after that."

"Good idea," says Ms. Oliverio. "And I'll sweeten the prize. Whoever finds the most *interesting* piece of garbage will receive one Get Out of a Pop Quiz Free card for science class."

"I'll throw in a Shakespeare action figure," says Mr. Van Deusen.

"Woo-hoo!" shouts Kwame. "Game on."

We each grab our own bags and start snagging litter so fast you'd think we'd just guzzled a gallon of coffee.

Siraj's trash bag is the heaviest, so he wins the fifteen minutes free (but he pitches in during the next burst of cleaning anyhow). Kwame wins the Skip a Pop Quiz card. He found a giant stuffed purple panda.

Fifteen minutes later, with one more pop quiz freebie on the line and everybody snagging trash as fast as they can, we're done. Tim's our final winner. He found a dented trombone.

"Um, I'm not in your class this term," he tells Ms. Oliverio.

"Well, I'll hold it over until next term," she says. "You guys did such a great job!"

"Kudos to you all," adds Mr. Van Deusen.

"Props to Piper," says Kwame. "She came up with the master plan."

"She should be president of the Chumley Prep Social Awareness Club," adds Siraj.

"Do we have one of those?" asks Kwame.

"We can start one!" says Tim. "Right, Ms. Oliverio?"

"It's fine by me," she says. "Mr. Van Deusen and I will even be your faculty advisors. Right, Schaack?"

"Will there be coffee?"

"Definitely," says Ms. Oliverio.

"Then I'm in."

All of a sudden, my mind starts whirring with ideas. I'm kind of excited.

"We could pick other causes, too," I say. "We could volunteer at homeless shelters and food banks. Or teach kids math. Or play board games at Mrs. Gilbert's senior citizen complex and walk rescue dogs at the animal shelter . . ."

"I nominate Piper for president," says Tim.

"I second that nomination," says Kwame. "All in favor, say 'Aye, matey.'"

"Huh?"

"It's more fun than plain old 'aye.'"

Everyone says "Aye, matey," and just like that, I'm president of a brand-new club.

And to tell you the truth, I don't really care if it impresses the Excelsior judges.

Doing good just feels good.

So I want to do more of it.

WHO DO I WANT TO BE?

Someone who always finds a way to do good. Nellie DuMont Frissé says, "Leave this planet better than you found it." But that's not going to happen unless people chip in and help. And I want to be one of those people.

CONNECTING THE DOTS

As we drive to school the next morning, Dad is beaming with pride.

"President of the Social Awareness Club?" he says with a smile.

"Yeah. We're going to have a meeting. First thing this morning."

"Social activism is the kind of thing your mother used to do."

"Really?"

"Yep. When we were in college at Michigan."

"But everybody always talks about what a great cello player she was."

"She was. But, honey, nobody is just one thing. We're like those constellations you're always telling me about. You need to connect all the dots to see the whole picture."

Wow. Interesting. I let that sink in.

"Hey," says Dad, "guess who called me?"

"Who?"

"Mr. Breckenridge."

"Brooke's dad?"

"Yep. Remember how he came up to me at the science fair reception and we talked about my music? Turns out, he's seriously considering talking to those New York City investors he advises. He's going to recommend that a group of them finance a workshop production of *Dream Time*."

"Wow," I say, wondering if maybe Dad was right: Chumley Prep could turn out to be the best thing to ever happen to both of us. "That's amazing!"

"I know!"

We park in our spot (it now has Dad's name painted over Mr. Glass's). Dad's phone buzzes. He glances at the screen.

"I have to run," he says. "Dr. Throckmorton wants to discuss an 'extremely urgent matter.'"

"See you later!" I shout as he sprints across the parking lot.

I dash up the front steps and head for the media center. I want to organize my "social awareness" thoughts before the rest of the gang shows up for a quick fifteen-minute "next steps" meeting. We need to pick our next activity. Figure out what we should do first.

Knowing how much Mister Pugsly means to Mrs. Gilbert, I'm pumped about a project called Seniors for Seniors. The idea is to match people over sixty with dogs over seven—the hardest ones to find homes for.

I've already sent an email to PAWS, a group in Washington State that runs a similar program. I'm hoping they'll help us kick-start our own Seniors for Seniors adoption program. I also talked to Mrs. Gilbert. She set up a meeting for me with the activities director at her senior citizen complex. Hopefully, I can convince them to work with us. Maybe I should take Mister Pugsly with me.

"Hello, *Piper Milly*."

Ainsley strolls into the media center. She sees the three-ring binder I made last night. It has a big CHUMLEY PREP SOCIAL AWARENESS CLUB sign tucked into the clear plastic sleeve on its cover.

"So it's true," Ainsley sneers.

"What's true?"

"You and those other dorky nerds had so much fun picking up trash along the side of the road, you decided to start your own club."

"Yes. We did. We have faculty sponsors, too."

"So do I."

"Excuse me?"

"Didn't you hear the news? I was elected president of the Chumley Prep Philosophy Club. My friends and I started it a few minutes ago."

"Is that really a thing?"

"It's as much of a thing as your 'social awareness society' or whatever you call it. I'm sure Mrs. Zamick will be *our* faculty advisor. Oh, by the way: if you think a fake presidency of a fake club is going to help you win the Excelsior Award . . ."

"What? That's not why we started the club."

Ainsley smirks. "You're wasting your time. Ten days from now, I will be the one taking home the Excelsior and you'll just be nobody. In case you didn't hear, I excelled at lacrosse yesterday. I was the MVP. They gave me a trophy and everything. Tomorrow I'll ace the forensics competition. Mrs. Zamick is the faculty advisor for that club, too. She wants us to do persuasive arguments."

"Sounds interesting . . ."

"It is. It's also for club members only. And guess what? Membership is closed!"

I smile and nod and scratch "Forensics Club" off the mental list of activities I might try to excel at to impress the Excelsior judges.

Because it's hard to excel at something when you can't even join the club.

*

*

EVENT HORIZON

After Ainsley makes her grand, strutting exit from the media center, my friends show up.

We have our fifteen-minute meeting and everybody agrees the Seniors for Seniors idea would be a great next project. They also like my official-looking binder.

"Let's find a local animal shelter to work with," suggests Emily.

I nod. "One with older dogs they're having trouble finding homes for."

The motion carries unanimously.

We divvy up the tasks and head to our homerooms. I'm not even thinking about Ainsley or the Excelsior Award, because I'm having too much fun thinking about all those rescue dogs making dozens of Mrs. Gilberts happy.

But then I go visit Dad during my independent study time.

He tells me about his meeting with Dr. Throckmorton.

"It was for all the music and performing arts teachers. There have been so many complaints from parents—including, of course, the Braden-Hammerschmidts and Mr. Breckenridge—that they've decided to do the spring talent show early this year. On March fourteenth."

"That's next week," I say. "One night before the Excelsior Award winner is announced."

"Exactly," says Dad. "It seems that talent will likely play a major role in the Excelsior judges' final deliberations."

Welp, I think, *buh-bye, Excelsior Award.*

Even if Siraj was right, that I was "in the lead" because I won the science fair, that lead has vanished. There are clear-cut winners at talent shows—just like there were at the athletic competitions.

"But I don't have a talent," I mutter.

"Sure you do, kiddo. Your talent is making me proud."

I arch my eyebrows. That is such a Dad-ish thing for him to say.

"Maybe I could learn how to juggle. . . ."

"Just keep doing your best, hon. That's all any of us can do."

I slump off to my next class.

Dr. Throckmorton makes the big talent show announcement over the PA system.

"Yes!" we hear Ainsley shout from the room across the hall. "I'm going to crush it!"

I slump to lunch with my friends.

Kwame and Tim are both thrilled that the spring talent show has been moved up.

"They've already asked me to emcee again," says Kwame. "I need to start working up some fresh material."

"Can the emcee win the talent show?" asks Emily.

"He can if he's as funny as I am! I get a full five minutes to do a comic monologue at the top of the show."

"I don't care about winning," says Tim. "I just want my dad to see me saw a lady in half."

"You think he'll be there?" I ask.

"I really hope so," says Tim.

"He's gonna love your new trick, Tim," I say.

"Maybe I could solve a complex equation at a rolling chalkboard," says Emily. "That would really wow the crowd."

After Kwame and Siraj finish lunch and leave the table, Tim turns to Emily. "Are you really going to do math for the talent show?" he asks.

"Um, no."

"Then maybe you could be the legs of the lady I saw in half."

"What?"

"Don't tell anybody, but I need *two* helpers to do the trick. Piper will be the one onstage with me, and—"

"Excuse me, *Piper Milly?*"

It's Ainsley. She's baaaaaack.

"Dr. Throckmorton needs to see us."

"Us?"

She nods and smiles. "It's about the science fair."

CRASHING TO EARTH

I'm sitting in Dr. Throckmorton's office, sinking into a padded leather chair, facing the headmaster's hulking desk.

Ainsley is perched on the edge of her matching chair. Smiling.

"Miss Milly?" says Dr. Throckmorton, his hands forming a thoughtful pyramid underneath his nose.

"Yes, sir?"

"Question: Did you read all the rules and regulations regarding this year's science fair exhibits?"

"To be honest, I sort of skimmed them. . . ."

"We didn't," says Ainsley.

We? I wonder.

She, of course, clarifies.

"My father's lawyers went through those rules with a fine-tooth comb."

"Miss Milly," says Dr. Throckmorton, looking extremely stern behind his owl glasses, "in the future, you would do well to familiarize yourself with all the rules and regulations governing any competition you might choose to enter. I call your attention to section twelve, 'use of firearms and weapons in science fair projects.'"

"Weapons?"

"You had a marble shooter!" says Ainsley. "A robot with a trigger that shot glass projectiles. It was a cannon! You could've put somebody's eye out with that thing."

"B-b-but—"

Dr. Throckmorton shows me the palm of his hand.

I don't think I'm allowed to protest whatever decision he's already made.

"According to section twelve, and I quote: 'To ensure the safety of the student and any people or animals in the vicinity of the project, a student with a project using firearms or other weapons must have a Research Advisor approve his/her plans *prior* to using the weapon.' Did you receive this prior approval, Miss Milly?"

"No," I say. "But Ms. Oliverio shot a marble at my moonscape. Does that count?"

Dr. Throckmorton shakes his head. Slowly.

"You leave me no choice, Miss Milly," the headmaster continues. "Since you violated the rules of the competition, we must rescind your first-place victory."

"That means they're taking away your blue ribbon," says Ainsley, pretending she's being helpful. "You didn't win. You lost."

"B-b-but . . . ," I sputter.

"Do you wish to formally protest Dr. Throckmorton's decision?" asks Ainsley in her phony helpful voice. "Maybe you should talk it over with your father first."

Dr. Throckmorton flips open a binder to study a color-coded chart. "I believe Mr. Milly has a free period coming up. . . ."

In a stomach-lurching flash, my mind races back to Christmas Eve.

The parents of the a cappella kids more or less forced their old director, Mr. Glass, into an early retirement. A bunch of parents angry about me could probably do the same thing to Dad.

And Dr. Throckmorton would be on the parents' side. Especially the superrich ones. The ones who donate money to the school. The ones who build the school its auditoriums and stadiums.

"I don't see any reason to involve my father," I say. "I'll tell him what happened."

"Wise decision," says Ainsley.

"I hope this experience has taught you a very valuable lesson," says Dr. Throckmorton.

It sure did, I think. The next time I go up against Ainsley Braden-Hammerschmidt, I need to bring my own team of lawyers.

"The science fair results will be officially adjusted," Dr. Throckmorton continues. "The three recipients of honorable mention ribbons—Siraj Shah, Emily Bleiberg, and, of course, Ainsley Braden-Hammerschmidt—shall be declared the three co-winners."

"Maybe we should have a runoff," suggests Ainsley. "Sudden-death overtime?"

"No," says Dr. Throckmorton. "I consider this matter closed."

Ainsley shrugs. "Fine. I'll crush it at the talent show."

She doesn't really seem to care about winning the science fair. She's just happy that my title's been taken away.

And that, now, I definitely don't stand a chance at winning the Excelsior Award.

THE FAULT IS NOT
IN OUR STARS

"I didn't know the robot was against the rules," I tell Dad when I finally see him after school.

"I guess we should've read them as closely as Ainsley and her father's lawyers did."

We're driving home in a dreary drizzle.

"Piper?"

"Yeah?"

"I'm sorry I don't have lawyers like Mr. Braden-Hammerschmidt."

"That's okay. He probably can't play the piano."

"Probably not. But he could hire someone to play it for him. Heck, he could hire a whole orchestra. . . ."

An ugly thought creeps into my mind.

This is all Tim's fault.

Tim's the one who insisted that I use his marble-shooting robot. He's the one who looked so sad when I told him I didn't need it. He's the one who made me break the rules I didn't read but probably should've.

This is definitely all Tim's fault.

"I guess I won't win the Excelsior Award next week," I say when we pull into our driveway.

"Sorry, kiddo," says Dad.

Then we just sit there.

"Whoever wins first place in the talent show will probably win the Excelsior Award, too," I say.

Dad nods. "Maybe. Are you thinking of entering it?"

"I was going to do a magic act with Tim," I tell Dad. "He was going to saw me in half."

"Tim's the one who gave you the robot marble shooter, right?"

"Yeah" is all I say, but I'm thinking: *THIS IS ALL HIS FAULT! TIM WAS MAD AT ME??? I'M THE ONE WHO SHOULD BE MAD AT HIM!!!*

Tim made me lose the science fair *and* the Excelsior Award!

If I do a stupid magic trick with him at the talent show,

it will just remind everybody about why I was disqualified and why I had my blue ribbon ripped away.

"By the way," says Dad, "I'm helping Brooke prep for the show."

"That's great," I say.

"She's the only student who asked. She wants to do one of the tunes I've been tinkering with for my musical. You know, 'Maybe Tomorrow.' It really shows off her vocal range. . . ."

I'm only half listening to Dad.

Because I realize that Hannah was right all along. Ainsley Braden-Hammerschmidt and Brooke Breckenridge are from a different galaxy than the one mere mortals like me inhabit. Those girls are superbrilliant stars you could see blazing from a billion light-years away.

Me?

I really don't have a talent to show the world.

I'm like that theoretical brown dwarf star or gas giant planet lurking at the far edges of our solar system, way beyond Pluto.

Nobody can see it.

Some doubt that it's even there.

BREAKING UP THE MAGIC ACT

That night, I text Tim to let him know that I won't be assisting him onstage at the talent show.

> You'll have to find somebody else to saw in half.

Then I give him the angry-face emoji and type in screaming all caps:

> YOU MADE ME LOSE THE SCIENCE FAIR AND THE EXCELSIOR AWARD!!!!

"Sorry," Tim texts back. "I didn't mean to do either of those things."

Later, Hannah comes over.

"Since when did you start reading Shakespeare?" she asks, after poking through the books on my desk.

"Oh, there's this teacher at Chumley Prep . . ."

She nods. "Like in that movie. Prep school teachers *love* dead poets. It's a thing."

"I guess. Anyway, there's this competition for something called the Excelsior Award."

"They're giving away Alka-Seltzer?"

"No, Hannah. It's for the student who excels the most during the winter term. I never really thought I had a shot. But then I won the science fair and people started telling me that I could win the big award, too. I started believing them."

"Seriously?" says Hannah. "But those rich kids excel at everything. And the ones who don't? They can pay people to excel for them!"

The car ride to school the next morning is extremely quiet. Neither Dad nor I say a word. He's not even humming any show tunes.

I figure he's quiet because he's feeling sorry for me. I'm quiet because I know I've let everybody down. Siraj and the others were really counting on me to win one for the Hibbleflitts team.

I avoid Tim all day.

I'm still angry at him and his dumb robot.

I do congratulate Siraj and Emily on their new status as science fair co-winners.

"It is a Pyrrhic victory at best," says Siraj.

He reads the *Huh?* on my face.

"It is a hollow victory," he explains. "Achieved at too great a cost on spurious grounds."

My face is *huh*ing again, so Emily jumps in.

"Ainsley's complaints were not genuine or true. That toy marble shooter wasn't a weapon. You should appeal Dr. Throckmorton's decision."

"And who would she appeal to?" asks Siraj. "Dr. Throckmorton is the headmaster. That means he is the *head*. There is no higher authority. His word is law."

I learn that Siraj has agreed to help Tim do his sawing-a-lady-in-half trick.

"I'm going to be the feet," he tells me. "I just have to wear the exact same socks and shoes as Emily. She's going to do your part."

I just nod.

After school on Friday, everyone is scurrying off to different rooms and rehearsal spaces to work on their acts for the talent show.

I'm hurrying along, too—mostly because I just want to go home and curl up in a ball on my bed.

As I'm heading up the halls, I come across a woman

who's rummaging around in a big rubber garbage barrel.
She's also sobbing.

And, of course, I have to stop and see what's wrong.

"This is the worst day of my life!" she says.

All I can think is *Join the club*.

A BARREL OF NOT LAUGHS

"I'm Ms. Rhodes," the lady tells me through sobs and sniffles. "I'm a substitute."

Kids keep streaming past us.

"I lost my grandmother's antique bracelet in the trash! The clasp broke, and the whole thing slipped off!"

"You sure it didn't just fall on the floor?" I ask.

"No. I heard it plunk against rubber. It's in the trash but I can't find it!"

I check out the garbage in the barrel. I see several greasy black banana peels. And brown apple cores. And lots of those plastic coffee drink domes smeared with whipped cream and smudges of caramel sauce glop.

I sigh, take off my blazer, roll up my sleeves, and go to work.

I dig deep but I can't find the bracelet. I have no choice. I have to, more or less, crawl into the barrel, headfirst.

I shove aside a layer of crumpled coffee cups and a napkin filled with the crumbs of a half-eaten blueberry muffin. I dig through those blackened banana peels. I try not to breathe.

Finally I see the bracelet. It's coated with mashed mush but it's okay!

"Got it!"

I give it to Ms. Rhodes.

"Thank you!" she gushes.

"You're welcome."

Hugging the bracelet tight, Ms. Rhodes hurries off, probably to find a jewelry shop that does bracelet repair and cleaning.

"Miss Milly?"

It's Mrs. Zamick.

"Why aren't you wearing your blazer?"

"Well, I—"

"And why is your blouse untucked?"

I start slipping the tails of my white shirt back under my skirt. Climbing into that trash barrel made me look like a mess.

"Do you think the dress code applies to everyone except you?"

"I was just trying to help a substitute teacher who—"

Mrs. Zamick shakes her head. "Just like your mother. You're so *special*."

"No, really, I was just—"

"You're lucky school is officially over for the day; otherwise I would write you up for violating the Chumley dress code."

"Yes, ma'am."

"Go to the girls' room, Miss Milly. Pull yourself together. And while you're in there, please wash up. You smell like a trash bin."

ABSOLUTE ZERO

I go into the bathroom.

Ainsley's at the mirrors, touching up her makeup—packing her arsenal of cosmetics into a designer tote bag.

"Oh, are you here to clean another toilet? Or do you plan on going dumpster diving again? I saw you with your head buried in the trash barrel. I totally Instagrammed your butt."

At that moment, I'm kind of glad I don't really do social media.

"Today will be a sweet, sweet victory for me," Ainsley continues. "In ten minutes, I'll be winning the Forensics Club competition, where, hello, I am totally going to crush it. Next Thursday is the talent show, where, of course, I will emerge victorious. And then next Friday will be even sweeter. That's when Dr. Throckmorton and the Chumley family will be handing me the first-ever Excelsior Award."

"Congratulations," I say, trying hard not to sound as defeated as I feel.

"Congratulations to you, too, Piper. It sounds like you've finally accepted your fate. It's always wise to quit while you're behind."

She laughs and exits the bathroom.

Leaving a stack of pink notecards on the sink.

They're sitting right there.

I can't resist.

I pick them up.

It's her entire speech.

For the Forensics Club competition.

Without her pink cards, Ainsley Braden-Hammerschmidt won't know what to say. She had to use notecards to tell the judges about her science project. They're like her crutch.

I read what she's written.

Seems she's picked an excellent topic, especially since Mrs. Zamick is the main judge for the forensics competition. Ainsley's planning on persuasively arguing that "For her hard work and dedication, Mrs. Patricia Zamick should be named teacher of the year at Chumley Prep."

But if Ainsley doesn't have her cards, she'll freeze. I know she will.

Is this my lucky day?

These cards could help me sabotage Ainsley the way Ainsley sabotaged me after the science fair.

I am so tempted to tear up her precious notes and flush them down the toilet.

But then, the toilet would probably get clogged. And water would pour all over the floor. And that poor janitor's next panic attack would be on me.

I also remember what I've written in my journal for Mr. Van Deusen.

Do I really want to become Ainsley?

I make up my mind.

I know what I have to do.

I grab the cards.

RETROGRADE ORBIT

I take them to Ainsley out in the hall.

"Here," I say. "You forgot your notes."

Ainsley eyes me suspiciously.

"Did you rearrange them? Shuffle them up?"

"I didn't do anything," I tell her. "I'm just taking your suggestion. I'm quitting while I'm behind."

Over the weekend, Dad can see I'm feeling sort of down.

I think that's why he made pancakes for breakfast. The kind with chocolate chip smiley faces. They're usually my fave, but I'm not really hungry. So I just cut them into wedges and push them around the plate, like syrup sponges.

"Hey, I have a great idea," he says, trying to cheer me up. "After breakfast, let's go to the animal shelter. You can get started on your Seniors for Seniors project. You want to do that today?"

I shrug. "Not really."

"Well, the paper says there's a new show at the planetarium! Nellie DuMont Frissé is the narrator."

I nod.

"Piper? You love the planetarium. You love Dr. Frissé. What could be better than this?"

"Not today, Dad. Maybe some other time."

"Sure, kiddo. Another time would be great."

I'm glad I spoke up for myself. I just wish I had something better to speak up about.

I walk Mister Pugsly. Twice on Saturday. Twice on Sunday.

He stares at me with his big, buggy eyes.

I think he feels sorry for me, too.

I call Hannah. But she's not home. Her mother tells me she went to the mall with her "new friend" Kaitlyn. I don't leave a message.

At night, it's so cloudy, there are no stars in the sky, only fog. I think even Ursa Major has taken the weekend off.

Monday morning, Dad and I drive back to Chumley Prep.

This is, of course, the first day of the final week before the winner of the Excelsior Award is announced. The talent show is scheduled for Thursday night, the award presentation for Friday morning. We assume the judges will huddle after the big show (the one I won't be in) and make their final decisions.

"There's always next year, hon," says Dad, because that's the Dad-ish thing to say when your daughter, more or less, sulks through an entire weekend.

"So how does Brooke sound on your song?" I ask. She and Dad rehearsed together three times over the weekend.

"Amazing. The girl has 'it,' you know what I mean?"

Yep. I do.

"So I guess there never really was any way I could've beaten her, huh?" I say.

Dad doesn't answer. Instead, he does what dads do. He changes the subject.

"Hey—I have an idea. Why don't you help me help Brooke?"

"How?"

"Become my assistant again. You know—like when you helped me at the a cappella contest."

"Sure," I say. "Why not? I've got nothing better to do this week."

"Atta girl!"

I find out from Siraj and Emily that their rehearsals with Tim are going "great."

"Tim saws me in half while Beethoven's Fifth Symphony triumphantly blares on a boom box," says Emily.

"We think the judges will be impressed," adds Siraj.

"We also think you and Tim should kiss and make up," says Emily. "Well, not the kissing part. That's just a figure of speech. . . ."

"We're the Hibbleflitts, Piper," adds Siraj. "We need to stick together."

I know they're right.

But I'm still feeling sorry for myself.

After classes, I head over to the PAC.

I'm right back where I started. I'm Dad's gofer. Going for this, going for that, going for whatever Brooke needs to sing and sound her best.

"Mr. Milly?" Brooke says, sort of sheepishly. "Yesterday my father told me he doesn't want me singing a show tune."

"But it shows off your voice beautifully."

"I know. It's why I picked your song in the first place. But my father thinks I should sing '*O Mio Babbino Caro.*' He says it's much more important."

Dad nods. "It is."

"Is that the caliber of song they might sing at Juilliard or the Academy of Vocal Arts in Philadelphia?"

"Probably. But you're only in middle school, Brooke."

"My father says it's never too early to plan for the future."

"Of course. I understand."

Dad leaves the room to go find the "*O Mio Babbino Caro*" sheet music in his office.

Brooke coughs a little.

"You need water," I say.

"Thanks," says Brooke when I hand her a bottle of room-temperature water. "Your dad is pretty awesome."

"Yeah," I say. "He truly is."

I'm guessing Brooke's father never makes her smiley-face pancakes to try to cheer her up.

Dad comes back in with the music.

"I'm sorry about this, Mr. Milly," says Brooke. "I'd rather do your song, but my father . . ."

"That's all right," says Dad. "We'll save my piece for when we do the show."

Poor Dad.

I wish I could say or do something to make him feel better. Because I think Brooke's father is making Dad feel like me.

And right now that's not much fun.

*　　*　　*

*

*

*

TALENT QUEST

That night over dinner, which we have at a fast-food place because Brooke kept us rehearsing *"O Mio Babbino Caro"* forever, I tell Dad how Tim, Siraj, and Emily are all working together in the talent show.

"Good for them," he says. "Do they know that Dr. Throckmorton wrote up some new rules?"

"Which you read very, very carefully?"

"You bet I did."

"So what are they?"

"Every student can only appear in one act. Dr. Throckmorton doesn't want anybody trying to impress the Excelsior judges by appearing onstage two or three different times."

"I don't think any of my friends are all that interested

in the Excelsior Award anymore," I say. "They just want to help Tim."

We finish our food and head for home.

The skies have cleared. I can see the stars.

Ursa Major is up there, right where she's supposed to be—protecting her daughter.

Or maybe she's nudging her. In fact, if you look at the arrangement of the two constellations a little differently, it's almost like Mama Bear sent Baby Bear spinning with a good swift head butt.

All of a sudden, I'm saying something out loud that doesn't sound like me saying it:

"I really wish I could do something in the talent show."

"You can, honey," says Dad. "It's not too late."

"But I'd never win."

"You might. Hey, you might even win the Excelsior Award."

"That's a bad hypothesis, Dad."

"I don't know, kiddo. Some of the teachers have been grumbling about Dr. Throckmorton's decision to disqualify your science fair victory."

"You really think I have a chance?"

"It's a possibility, Piper. What's that famous quote Nellie DuMont Frissé always says?"

"'Shoot for the moon. Even if you miss, you'll land among the stars.'"

"Exactly!"

"But what can I do for the talent show?"

"You're smart. Forget about what everybody else does so well. Singing. Dancing. Playing the ukulele. Do what *you're* good at! Do something you love."

Nellie DuMont Frissé always says the darkest nights produce the brightest stars.

Boy, is this night dark.

I rack my brain till way past midnight and I still can't think of any talent I could possibly perform on a stage alongside superstars like Brooke or Ainsley or Kwame or even the Great Timdini.

I make a quick entry to my project for Mr. Van Deusen:

WHO DO I WANT TO BE?

Someone who doesn't give up.

The next morning, Dad is on the computer in the kitchen.

"I got us tickets," he says. "Next month."

"Great. Um, where are we going?"

"To see 'Journey into the Unknown.' The new show at the planetarium I told you about."

"Oh. Cool."

He starts reading the blurb. "'It's an incredible voyage to the far reaches of our known universe, exploring . . .'"

Yes, Dad's talking and I'm distracted again. Because, all of a sudden, I realize: I *do* have a talent.

One that I know nobody else will be bringing to the stage on Thursday night because it's not usually considered, you know, a talent in the traditional sense.

Astronomy!

I just have to find some way to make it as entertaining as a cello solo, an operatic aria, or a magic trick. I have to make it as spectacular as a Nellie DuMont Frissé show at the planetarium!

I can't just spend my time gazing up at the stars.

I need to become one.

*

*

STARS IN MY EYES

"I think it's fantastic," says Ms. Oliverio when I tell her my idea for the talent show. "Go for it, Piper! Shine on, stargazer! Shine on!"

I decide to not give up on Tim, either. We sit together at lunch for the first time since I sent him that angry-face emoji.

"I'm sorry I blamed you for the whole science fair thing," I tell Tim, who's looking down at the dining hall floor. "I guess I was just mad, and you made an easy target."

"I'm very sorry it turned out the way it did," he replies without looking up. "I was trying to help."

"You did help," I tell him. "You gave my science project pizzazz. It needed pizzazz."

Finally he looks me in the eye. I see that small smile creep across his face again, and it makes me smile, too.

"Pizzazz," says Kwame. "Sounds like what would happen if pizza and jazz got married. . . ."

"Ainsley robbed you, Piper," says Siraj.

"Well, don't worry," says Emily. "On Thursday night, revenge will be ours. Timothy Bartlett shall transform into the Great Timdini! His magic act will crush Ainsley's cello piece."

"Actually," says Tim, "Ainsley's very good. I've heard her rehearsing in the PAC."

"But you will amaze and astound your audience," says Emily. "You will be fantabulous!"

"You just made up that word, right?" cracks Kwame.

"Maybe," Emily admits.

A laugh goes around the table. It feels good to be with friends again.

"I suspect," says Siraj, "that the talent show will come down to three or four top contenders."

"Me, of course," says Kwame.

"Yes, I would put you in the top tier."

"Appreciate that, Siraj."

"Then Brooke, and that sixth grader with the guitar I heard rehearsing in the stairwell, and, of course, the Great Timdini."

Everybody nods. No one wants to admit that Ainsley has an excellent chance at winning . . . everything!

"Guess what?" I say. "I'm thinking about doing something scientific for the talent show."

"Like what?" asks Kwame. "Juggling to show how atomic particles and molecules work?"

"No. Something about the stars. Maybe something like Nellie DuMont Frissé does. I'm going to buy a star projector and talk about the constellations."

After school, when Dad finishes working with Brooke, he drives me to the electronics store, where I spend all of my dog-walking money to buy a pretty expensive (and super-impressive) Homestar Planetarium Projector.

That night I duct-tape black trash bags over the garage windows so no light can leak in. I beam a field of stars against a dark blue sheet I hang off Dad's tool pegboard. It's pretty cool. Sort of like stargazing outdoors—minus the mosquitoes.

I choose the projector disc that shows Ursa Major, of course.

Inside that constellation is another one—the Big Dipper. You can use the Big Dipper to find Polaris, the North Star, which, by the way, is the tail end of the handle of the Little Dipper. The two stars forming the outer edge of the bowl of the Big Dipper are named Merak and Dubhe and are known as the pointers, because if you draw an imaginary line between them, it'll point you north to Polaris.

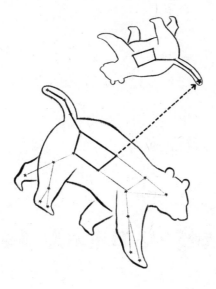

That's right, Big Mama Bear is always showing the whole world how to, no pun intended, find its bearings.

It hits me.

This is what my act should be about!

Finding the North Star, which is how everybody from the Egyptians to the Vikings to the Polynesians was able to chart their courses across unknown seas.

Even Shakespeare (thank you, Mr. Van Deusen) wrote about how constant the North Star is in his play *Julius Caesar.*

Shakespeare!

If I quote him, my star projector act will be as classy as a cello solo!

STARS IN THE GARAGE

During school on Wednesday, I scope out how the auditorium will be set up for Thursday evening's talent show.

There's a big black curtain hanging across the back of the stage. It's perfect for projecting a few billion stars.

Next, I write my script.

I find some dramatic music, including the song "We Know the Way" from Disney's *Moana*. The lyrics are perfect:

> *At night, we name every star*
> *We know where we are*
> *We know who we are*

Knowing who you are? That's probably even more important than knowing where you are.

Because if you know who you are before you set off on a journey, you'll probably have a better idea about where you want to go. (I wonder if Mr. Van Deusen has ever seen *Moana*.)

After school, Dad does one last "dress rehearsal" with Brooke. Her "*O Mio Babbino Caro*" sounds amazing, but I'm sort of bored with it. I've only heard her sing it a bajillion times.

We head for home. After we both gobble down a quick microwaved dinner, I invite Dad into the garage to see my show. He will be my first audience.

He sets up a folding aluminum chair in front of the garage doors and applauds as I take the stage on the oil-stained concrete floor.

"Welcome, stargazers," I say, feeling giddy but not the least bit nervous, because talking about stars is my happy place. "Tonight we will go on a journey—without a map or a GPS. Tonight we will travel using only the stars to guide us!"

I flick on the projector and flood the dark blue sheet with a spectacular swirled sea of stars. Dad oohs. It's hard not to when you see that many stars.

"Finding our way under the night sky is a galaxy-sized version of a connect-the-dots game!"

I turn up the volume on my soundtrack. I've edited together some very dramatic stuff, most of it from movies.

I tell a quick tale about Viking and Egyptian explorers traveling across the oceans. When my music shifts to the *Moana* song, I talk about how the Polynesians followed maps in the stars.

"They looked at the sky differently than most people and used celestial navigation to become the world's greatest explorers. They were wayfinders, working with a thousand points of light in the sky to find their way to the islands dotting the Pacific!"

And then I go into the interactive portion of my program.

"But how do we use the stars when we wish to journey safely into the vast unknown? It's simple, really. We just need to find one star. Polaris. The North Star. The one that's always constant and true. If we know where north is, then we know where south, east, and west are, too. Luckily, Polaris is always in the same spot in the sky. It is a constant, twinkling light above the North Pole."

Then I walk my audience through how they can find the North Star by first finding the Big Dipper inside Ursa Major and following the imaginary line between the two stars in the cup to reach Polaris at the tip of the ladle on the Little Dipper.

"Amazing!" says Dad.

Time for my big wrap-up.

"Yes, the stars can guide us. They can lead us. But it is up to each and every one of us to choose whether or not we will boldly go where others have feared to venture. It is up to us to decide who we will be in this grand journey called life. For, as Shakespeare once wrote, 'It is not in the stars to hold our destiny but in ourselves.' Thank you."

Dad leaps out of his lawn chair to give me a standing ovation.

"Bravo! Incredible!"

Wow!

Shooting for the moon is fun!

JITTERS

Thursday night.

Everybody is scurrying around backstage. The talent show starts in thirty minutes. There are so many nervous-energy particles buzzing through the air, we might create our own aurora borealis.

I'm wearing a black dress decorated with hot-glued glitter stars that I cut out of some old Christmas wrapping paper I found in my closet.

I hear Mrs. Braden-Hammerschmidt as Ainsley clicks open the locks on her cello case: "Crush it, Ainsley!"

"Yes, Mother," Ainsley snaps. "I've got it."

"Oh, you better hope you do, young lady."

For the first time ever, I see fear flicker in Ainsley's eyes. Her perfectness cracks—just a little.

"Yes, ma'am," she mutters. She looks like she wants to cry.

For a split second, I see her totally differently than I usually do. It's like those moon images again. I'm not seeing the Ainsley I expect.

Fortunately, parents aren't allowed backstage during the talent show (another one of Dr. Throckmorton's new rules).

"You'll be great," I whisper to Ainsley when her mother is gone. "You're an amazing musician."

Ainsley looks surprised but manages a soft "Thanks."

She drags her cello off to a darkened corner to warm up.

Our master of ceremonies, Kwame, is pacing back and forth in his tuxedo, flipping through his joke notebook.

"Has anybody seen the running order yet?" he calls out to nobody in particular. "Have they posted the list? How am I supposed to know who to make fun of first?"

"No list yet," says Siraj, who's standing next to Tim's rolling magic-trick box. Siraj is wearing red-striped socks and glistening ruby-red slippers. I guess that's what Emily's wearing, too.

Tim's in a top hat and tails.

"You look sharp," I tell him.

"So does his saw blade," quips Siraj.

"How's your act?" Tim asks me.

"My dad liked it," I tell him. "Of course, that was last night in the garage."

Tim peeks through the middle of the stage curtains. "I hope my dad likes mine."

"He's here?"

"Yep. Mom played the golf card. Dad either had to come to this or skip his golf trip on Saturday and go wallpaper shopping. It worked."

I hug Tim. I think it shocks him. But I hug him anyway.

"Um, okay. Thanks, Piper."

Kwame comes over. "Hey, did you guys hear about the violinist who played in tune?"

"No," Tim and I say.

"Yeah, neither did I," says Kwame.

We laugh. He jots down something in his notebook and paces away. "Definitely gonna use that one. . . ."

Tim holds back the curtain so I can look out into the audience.

"He's the one in the second row," says Tim. "In the suit and tie. He came straight from the office."

I see his father. He looks a little fidgety, but he's out there.

"I'm so glad he's here," I say.

"Yeah," says Tim. "Me too."

"Now we just need Emily," says Siraj.

"What?" I say. "Where is she?"

Siraj shrugs. "Running late, I guess."

"We should text her," says Tim, sounding nervous.

"Again?" says Siraj.

"Yes!"

"I'll text her," I say.

"Ladies and gentlemen? May I have your attention, please?"

A woman dressed all in black, wearing a headset and carrying a clipboard, comes to center stage behind the curtain. I figure she must be the stage manager in charge of running the show. Stage managers always have headsets and carry clipboards.

"For those of you who don't know me, my name is Avery Hessler and I'm the assistant drama teacher. I'll be your stage manager this evening."

Nailed it.

"Dr. Throckmorton asked that I repeat the rules of the competition," Ms. Hessler continues. "Here we go: All students can appear in one act and one act only. If you do a team performance, you win or lose together. You can't do a team act and then come back later as a soloist. Is everybody clear on that?"

Heads nod.

"Also, no parents, teachers, or coaches are allowed backstage. None. Okay. Here's the running order for the show."

She passes out copies and tapes one to the wall. There are two dozen different acts.

Kwame is up first with his opening monologue.

Then comes Brooke.

After Brooke come the eighth-grade ballet dancers.

Then a sixth-grade poet.

After the poet, "the Great Timdini."

Ainsley will do her cello piece right after Tim saws Emily in half.

And I'm on right after Ainsley.

Putting me in the perfect position to, hopefully, make everybody forget how brilliant she is on the cello and, maybe, just maybe, make this my night to shine!

A STAGE FULL OF STARS

The curtain goes up!

Kwame strolls onstage with a microphone to warm up the crowd.

"Welcome, everybody, to the spring talent show, even though it isn't officially spring for, what, six more days? But hey, this is Chumley Prep. If we want spring to arrive before March twentieth, we just pay it a little extra to show up early."

The audience laughs.

"Y'know, I've got nothing against millionaires. They're just like everybody else, only richer."

While Kwame keeps cracking jokes, I look around.

Brooke is waiting in the wings, eager to take the stage.

I've got my planetarium projector on a rolling cart. It's hooked up to a long extension cord. Tim and Siraj are right next to me with their magician's box.

Tim is panicking.

"Where's Emily?" I hear him mutter.

My phone vibrates. So do Tim's and Siraj's.

Emily's father has just answered all our texts:

> Emily won't be able to join you kids this evening. She had a bicycle accident. She sprained her wrist. We're at Urgent Care.

Tim looks like he might be ill.

Kwame introduces Brooke. She takes the stage and, once Dad is seated at the piano on the floor at the foot of the stage, launches into *"O Mio Babbino Caro."*

She is, of course, fantastic.

After she hits her last high note and holds it for forever, the audience gives her a standing ovation. She points to Dad at the piano. He stands, takes a bow. The audience starts screaming "Brava!" and "Bravo!"

Kwame returns to the stage. "Give it up for the one and only Brooke Breckenridge, everybody. You know what I like best about opera? When it's over."

Kwame brings on the next act, the eighth-grade ballet troupe.

Meanwhile, Tim is still freaking out.

"I can't do the trick without Emily!" he says.

"I could do her part," suggests Siraj.

"Then who'd do *your* part?" asks Tim. Sweat is bubbling up on his brow.

"What was Emily supposed to do?" I ask.

And, while the corps de ballet pirouettes and leaps across the stage, Tim breaks his magician's code and tells me exactly how the trick is done.

PRESTO CHANGO

Turns out, Tim's magic box has two separate compartments.

The "feet section" has a false bottom built into the rolling table the box is sitting on. That's where Siraj will hide his head, chest, and arms.

"I hide in the bottom and don't stick out my feet until I hear Emily climbing into the top," Siraj explains.

"Emily scrunches herself up in the top half, with her legs tucked tight to her chest," says Tim, his voice shaky. "But that's impossible now because she's not here. . . ."

The ballet troupe takes their bow. Kwame comes onstage to crack another joke.

"You know why dogs make such lousy ballerinas?" he asks the crowd. "Because they have two left feet."

He tells a few more one-liners and introduces a young kid dressed in black pants and a black turtleneck sweater. Apparently, he is the "poet laureate of the sixth grade."

Me? I'm standing in the wings next to Tim and Siraj, thinking.

About what's really important.

What's constant and true.

It's not just the North Star. It's friends. And family. And friends who become family.

I'm also thinking about Ursa Major, and how, if you let her, the Big Mama Bear in the sky will always point you in the right direction.

Or she might give you a gentle nudge.

I smile. Because I know what I need to do.

"Did Emily take home her socks and sparkly shoes?" I ask.

Tim shakes his head. "No. They're in the top of the box."

"Great." I kick off my shoes and start unrolling my socks.

"Um, what're you doing, Piper?" asks Tim.

"Taking Emily's place."

"But you can only be in one act," Siraj reminds me.

"I know." I slip on one shimmering ruby shoe and,

tugging on the other one, hop over to the control panel, where the stage manager is calling cues into her headset.

"Okay, cue Kwame," she says. "Let's get the poet off-stage. Twelve verses is enough. . . ."

"Ms. Hessler?" I whisper. "I'm Piper Milly."

She consults her clipboard. "Wait in the wings. You're on after Ainsley."

"I know. But I'm not going to do my solo act."

"What?"

"You can scratch me off the list. I'm going to do the magic act with Siraj and the Great Timdini. They need an assistant."

"You're giving up your own slot?"

"Yeah." I shrug. "It's what friends do."

THE GREAT TIMDINI!

"Oh-kay," says Kwame when the sixth-grade poet finally leaves the stage. "You know how poets sneeze? *Haiku!* Our next act is one of my personal favorites. Give it up for the magical stylings of the one and only, the Great Timdini!"

Tim rolls the box onto the stage. Siraj is hidden in his secret compartment. I carry Tim's MP3 player with the Beethoven music loaded on it down to the lip of the stage.

While the audience applauds for Tim, I strike various magician-assistant poses like the ones I've seen on TV. You know—one arm up, the other pointing game show–style at nothing in particular. My sparkly star dress looks very magician-assistant-ish, too.

Tim starts his spiel.

"Good evening, ladies and gentlemen, boys and girls. Prepare to be mesmerized, shocked, and astounded! For I am the Great Timdini! Piff-piff!"

I shift my pose. I basically just change which arm is pointing up and which one is pointing sideways. Tim pulls out some shiny steel rings for his first trick.

"Examine these rings closely," he says to me. "Do you see any holes?"

"No," I say.

"How about the big one in the center there?"

The audience laughs. Tim bangs the rings together and makes them pass through each other. While he does that, I glance around the auditorium. I see Ms. Oliverio. Mr. Van Deusen. And, down in the front row, Dad.

With his mouth hanging open.

He has a total "what the what?" look on his face.

He's just realized that I'm not going to win the talent show or the Excelsior Award. I am not going to see my name engraved on a plaque like Mom. I'm just going to be me—Piper Milly.

Focus on your friends, I tell myself. *They need you.*

Tim pulls his fluttering windup bird out of my hair and sends it flying out over the auditorium.

The audience laughs. They love the Great Timdini.

I cheat another sideways glance. Now I see Tim's father. The man is smiling, big-time.

Tim does a quick card trick with a volunteer from the audience, then returns to the stage to set up the main event.

"Sawing a lady in half," he says. "A classic of the magician's craft. A trick not to be attempted lightly."

He pulls a saw out of his long tailcoat. (That thing has some extremely deep pockets.)

"I dedicate this next trick to my father."

A spotlight swings over to where Tim is pointing. Mr. Bartlett looks a little surprised by the sudden attention, but he waves. The audience applauds. Everyone has a sense of how much this next trick means to the Great Timdini.

"Let's hope I don't goof up," says Tim, comically bending his sword and shooting me a worried look.

"I agree," I ad-lib.

Tim points to the box.

I walk over, lift the lid. From my vantage point, I can see Siraj hiding in the bottom. The audience, however, cannot.

I climb into the top half and pull my knees to my chest.

As I squeeze in, I can hear Siraj pushing his feet through the leg holes. Remember, his shoes and socks look just like mine. I stick my head out of the head hole. The trick is working.

Tim lowers the lid on the box, flicks some snaps. I'm locked in.

Next, he grandly marches to the lip of the stage and says, "Maestro, if you please?"

He pushes play on the MP3 player.

No Beethoven comes out. Not the Fifth Symphony, the Sixth, or the Seventh.

Nothing.

The trick isn't working anymore.

PANIC ATTACK

Tim pushes play again.

Still nothing.

He jabs it repeatedly.

More nothing.

"Guess we should've checked the battery!" I joke from my locked and frozen position inside the box.

"This is a disaster," I hear Tim mumble.

My legs are starting to cramp up.

"Surely the Great Timdini doesn't need music to make magic!" I say, trying my best to keep the act going.

"I need Beethoven's Fifth," Tim mutters.

"Forget the Fifth," I joke. "Just saw me in half."

The audience titters.

Tim doesn't.

"We rehearsed this and rehearsed this," he mumbles. "Over and over. Everything is timed out to the music. . . ."

OMG. Tim is having a major meltdown. Onstage. In the middle of the talent show. In front of his father.

"I'm sorry, Dad. . . ."

His whole body is trembling.

The audience goes completely quiet. I hear a few chairs squeak. One cough. That's it.

Then I see the silhouette of somebody standing up in the front row. Has the audience had enough? Are people starting to walk out on the Great Timdini?

"Do you require musical accompaniment, O Great Timdini?"

It's Dad! He's walking to the piano bench.

"Yes!" says Tim, snapping back, adjusting his top hat, and flicking out his coattails. "Beethoven's Fifth, if you please. Do you see what a magnificent magician I am, ladies and gentlemen? I just made a pianist appear out of thin air!"

And with that, the audience breathes a collective sigh of relief. Actually, they laugh, which is, basically, the same thing.

Dad bangs out the opening bars to Beethoven's Fifth.

Da-da-da-DUM!

Tim plays the beats. Sawing in time to the music. It's hysterical.

Da-da-da-DUM!

Dad keeps going, Tim keeps sawing.

Finally Tim slides the box apart. I have been cut in half!

The crowd goes wild! Tim is beaming!

When the applause starts to die down, Tim slides the box back together. He unclasps the latches and raises the lid. Siraj pulls in his feet and I pop up out of the box.

We get a standing ovation.

Tim's father is standing, too.

And he's clapping and cheering louder than anybody!

BYE-BYE, EXCELSIOR AWARD

I push the box offstage while Ainsley Braden-Hammerschmidt rolls her cello into the spotlight, where Tim is taking his sixth bow.

Kwame dashes onstage to ringmaster the proceedings.

"Let's hear it one more time for the Great Timdini."

Tim shakes Kwame's hand. And pulls a mile-long scarf out of Kwame's tux sleeve. The audience cracks up.

Ainsley clears her throat. Loudly.

Tim takes one last bow and bounds off the stage, happier than I've ever seen him. In the wings, I'm helping Siraj climb out of the bottom half of the box. He's a little wobbly. Both his legs fell asleep on him.

"Thanks, you guys!" says Tim.

"You had me worried," says Siraj, while Ainsley sets up her cello at center stage.

"Me too," I say.

"Sorry. Guess I freaked out a little. Good thing Piper's dad was out there."

"Yeah," I say.

I realize, Dad's kind of a North Star, too.

Ainsley plays a Bach sonata, which, it turns out, is a hauntingly beautiful cello piece. I know it is because that's how Ainsley introduces it.

"And now," she says, "the prelude to Johann Sebastian Bach's hauntingly beautiful Cello Sonata Number One in G."

More than a dozen acts later, including that sixth grader with the electric guitar (he really is amazing), half a dozen singers, some gymnastics, and a trombone solo, the talent show ends.

And just as Dad predicted, Brooke Breckenridge takes first place. Ainsley comes in second. Tim ties for third with that sixth grader with the guitar.

All sorts of parents and friends start streaming backstage after the winners are announced.

Dad is in the crowd.

I see him dabbing at his eyes with his handkerchief. I figure he's been weeping because I publicly blew my last chance at winning the Excelsior Award.

"I'm sorry I let you down, Dad," I tell him. "But Emily sprained her wrist and Tim needed help and his father—"

I stop yammering because Dad is shaking his head and smiling at me.

"I'm not crying because I'm upset, Piper. In fact, I don't think I've ever been prouder. When I see you do something like that, something exactly like your mother would've done, it makes me feel as if she's still here."

"But Mom played the cello. I didn't play the cello. That was Ainsley, Dad. . . ."

"Honey, your mom was a fantastic cello player. Yes. She had a talent. A gift, even. But that's not what made her the most fantastic person I'd ever met in my life. She was also incredibly kind. And incredibly smart. She was so generous, she would do anything for her friends, which made me the luckiest man on earth because, guess what? I got to be her best friend. And then? I got you!"

We hug.

"Well done, Mr. Milly," says Brooke's father as he comes over to shake Dad's hand. "Now then, as promised, we should discuss putting together a small group of backers to invest seed money in your show." He glances at his watch. "I have to fly out of town first thing tomorrow morning. I could, however, do a late supper tonight. . . ."

"Can I take a rain check?" says Dad. "I have a prior engagement this evening."

"Is that so?" says Mr. Breckenridge. "Well, if you're otherwise committed, a rain check it is." He drifts off to greet more well-wishers, taking Brooke with him. "Come along, dear. There are some very important people I want you to meet. . . ."

"You should've gone out with him, Dad," I say.

"Nope. You heard me. I have a prior commitment."

"With who?"

"My favorite person." He drapes his arm over my shoulder and walks me toward the exit. "So, kiddo, who makes the best hot fudge sundaes in town?"

"Mootown, I guess."

"Excellent choice."

So that's where we go after the show.

And over hot fudge sundaes (with whipped cream *and* marshmallows), Dad tells me all sorts of stories about my mom that he says he probably should've told me years ago.

I love hearing every single one of them.

HAPPY EXCELSIOR DAY!

Friday morning.

March 15.

We're all back in the Hammerschmidt Auditorium for the presentation of the big award.

Ainsley takes a seat in the front row. "So I don't have to walk too far when they announce the winner," she tells the girls in her gaggle. They all giggle and tell her, "You deserve it!"

She's really looking forward to winning the Excelsior. Me? I'm really looking forward to my meeting tomorrow with the activities director at Mrs. Gilbert's seniors' apartment complex. We're going to find a lot of loving homes for older dogs!

I'm sitting with Tim, Siraj, Emily (her wrist is wrapped in an Ace bandage), and Kwame.

"Hey," says Kwame. "Do you guys know how many Ainsley Braden-Hammerschmidts it takes to screw in a lightbulb?"

"One," says Tim.

"She holds it," says Siraj.

Emily finishes with the punch line: "And the whole world revolves around her."

"You got that right," says Kwame.

Dad comes in with the rest of the faculty. Mr. Van Deusen has another cup of coffee and half a chocolate doughnut. Looks like Ms. Oliverio has the other half. I see Mrs. Zamick beaming at Ainsley, her protégée. Dad is smiling at me proudly. He shoots me a wink. I wave back.

Dr. Throckmorton walks onstage.

The crowd—every sixth, seventh, and eighth grader at Chumley Prep—settles down.

"Ladies and gentlemen," says Dr. Throckmorton, "today is the big day. The awarding of the first-ever Excelsior Award. So, without any further ado, it is my great honor and privilege to present a member of the family that started this school over two centuries ago. I give you Chatsworth W. Chumley the Third."

Our headmaster gestures to the wings. A spry old man in a natty blue blazer scurries out to join him onstage.

Wait a second. . . .

I squint because I realize something: I recognize the man.

He's the Chumley Prep alumnus I saw at the a cappella competition. The one who scampered out of the shadows and said what I wish I could've said. The one who told the Chumley kids that they weren't the center of this or any other known universe.

Mr. Chumley shakes Dr. Throckmorton's hand and moves to the microphone.

"Thank you, Osgood. Good morning, children. It is indeed a pleasure to be with you all once again. Of all my family's accomplishments, founding this school has long been our proudest achievement. However, not too long ago, I attended an a cappella competition at the Municipal Auditorium where I was astonished and, frankly, quite embarrassed by the behavior of several Chumley Prep students."

I glance over at Ainsley. She looks a little nervous.

"Their disrespectful demeanor is why I decided that my family needed to sponsor a new kind of award. If we want to fulfill Chumley Prep's mission of helping each and every student become their best and most fully realized self, we must educate and inspire their hearts as well as their heads."

"What's going on, you guys?" whispers Emily.

"I have no idea," Siraj whispers back.

"We need to reset our focus on building character," Mr. Chumley continues. "What C. S. Lewis called 'doing the right thing even when no one is watching.' Or, in the case of the Excelsior Award, even when you *think* no one is watching."

I see Ainsley squirm in her seat. I don't think this is what she was expecting.

I know I sure wasn't.

MYSTERIES REVEALED

Mr. Chumley takes a sip of water from a drinking glass and continues.

"Even your headmaster, Dr. Throckmorton, had no idea about the true nature of this so-called competition. My undercover judges have witnessed many great accomplishments over the course of this winter term. Impressive test scores. Amazing musical performances. Fascinating scientific presentations. Impressive feats of prestidigitation. But, ladies and gentlemen, there was more to this competition than met the eye. You see, we weren't interested in your grades, how many offices you held, if you won a basketball game or even the talent show."

Now Ainsley slumps down in her seat.

"The Chumley family firmly believes that to excel in life, you must make a difference in the lives of those around you. The brightest stars don't just shine for themselves. That's why my colleagues and I created five small tests. You were all given an equal opportunity to participate in each of these five scenarios. We set them up, then waited and watched to see who among you responded with compassion and concern. Very well. Enough about all that. It's time to end the mystery and unveil my panel of undercover judges."

Everyone is on the edge of their seat.

"Who do you think they were?" Tim whispers.

"I have absolutely no idea," I whisper back.

"I wanted five judges so there couldn't be a tie when selecting our winner," Mr. Chumley continues. "That proved to be an unnecessary precaution. The judges' final decision was unanimous."

Mr. Chumley turns to his right. "Judges, please join me here at the podium as I call out your names. First up: Mrs. Kate Sullivan. Kindergarten teacher. She is joined today by her directionally challenged students, Abby and Victor."

A woman and two small children join Mr. Chumley onstage.

"When these two pretended to be lost in the halls of

the middle school, only two students dropped everything to offer assistance."

Tim elbows me.

"That was us!"

"Judge number two," says Mr. Chumley. "Judy Gaffney, one of our wonderful food service employees, who, on several occasions, accidentally-on-purpose dropped her tray in the dining hall."

The audience chuckles.

"Only one student came to Judy's aid in her time of need. Judge three: a very talented young actor named Steven Harris, who impersonated a custodian pleading for assistance after a plumbing disaster. One student rushed to his aid. Judge four: Cara Lingle, another actor. She impersonated a nanny who could carry more backpacks than any human being should ever be asked to carry. Only one student offered to help lighten her load. And finally judge five, my wonderful granddaughter, Mrs. Barbara Rhodes. She pretended to be a substitute teacher who'd lost a precious family heirloom in a garbage barrel. Again, only one student offered to help her retrieve it. And it was the same student who helped all the others."

My face is starting to feel warm. I remember all those people.

Mr. Chumley reaches under the podium and pulls out an engraved glass plaque.

"As I said, the judges were unanimous in their final

decision. Ladies and gentlemen, it gives me and the entire Chumley family great pleasure to present the first-ever Excelsior Award to the student who consistently displayed kindness, even in the most trying and unusual of circumstances: Miss Piper Milly!"

SHINE TIME!

I am totally stunned.

Which is probably why I'm still sitting in my seat when the audience starts applauding.

"Go on!" says Tim.

"Get up there!" says Siraj.

Emily's gesturing like crazy.

Kwame gives me a little shove. "Hurry up, Piper! If you don't pick up your prize sometime soon, they might cancel lunch."

Somehow, my legs work and I make my way to the stage.

Mr. Chumley shakes my hand and gives me the heavy engraved glass. The Excelsior Award.

"Congratulations, Miss Milly," says Mr. Chumley.

"Thank you, sir."

"A little birdie named Ms. Oliverio tells me you are a fan of Dr. Nellie DuMont Frissé?"

"Yes, sir. I am."

"Wonderful. My family's foundation is a proud sponsor of her program on PBS. You should go to a taping. How about I set it up?"

"That would be amazing, sir."

The audience applauds as, one by one, the judges come over and say "Congratulations!"

I see Dad in the audience. Yep. He's crying again.

"Would you like to say a few words?" Mr. Chumley whispers.

"Do I have to?"

Mr. Chumley laughs. "Of course not. What you did over these past few weeks tells me more about who you are than anything you could possibly say."

And so—phew—I don't have to make a speech.

I just have to stand there, at center stage, soaking up the applause. It feels pretty awesome.

And all of a sudden I know exactly what I'm going to write for Mr. Van Deusen.

I know who I want to be.

Me.

*

*

THANK YOU!

Writing this book together, we were very fortunate to have a third partner: our terrific editor, Shana Corey. We can never thank her enough for helping us find our true north.

Thanks again to Eric Myers, our amazing literary agent.

Thanks to all the fantastic folks who helped us shape and detail our story: Ben Frahm, Steven Harris, Kate John, and Dorian Rence. And of course we are forever grateful to our early readers: Sunshine, Lucy, J. D., and Micah Cavalluzzi; Lily Lawler; Hayden Unger; and Halle Webman.

We'd also like to thank everybody at Random House Children's Books who has been so supportive ever since we first floated the idea of writing a book together: John Adamo, Kerri Benvenuto, Julianne Conlon, Janet Foley, Judith Haut, Kate Keating, Jules Kelly, Gillian Levinson, Mallory Loehr, Barbara Marcus, Kelly McGauley, Michelle Nagler, Polo Orozco, and Janine Perez.

Thank you to Leslie Mechanic, our cover artist and

designer, and the entire RHCB art department, including Katrina Damkoehler, Stephanie Moss, Trish Parcell, and Martha Rago, for making *Shine!* shine.

We were very lucky to have a crack team of copyeditors (who even copyedited these thank-yous): Barbara Bakowski, Alison Kolani, and Barbara Perris.

So many other people at Random House have helped make this book possible:

The production crew, headed up by Tim Terhune.

The school and library marketing team: Shaughnessy Miller, Lisa Nadel, Emily Petrick, Kristin Schulz, Erica Stone, and Adrienne Waintraub.

Our pals in publicity: Dominique Cimina, Aisha Cloud, and Noreen Heritz.

And the sensational sales force, who do such a great job getting the right books into the right kids' hands: Emily Bruce, Brenda Conway, Dandy Conway, Whitney Conyers, Stephanie Davey, Nic DuFort, Cletus Durkin, Joe English, Felicia Frazier, Becky Green, Susan Hecht, Kimberly Langus, Ruth Liebmann, Lauren Mackey, Cindy Mapp, Deanna Meyeroff, Carol Monteiro, Tim Mooney, Sarah Nasif, Stacey Pyle, Mark Santella, Sophie Stewart, Kate Sullivan, Liz Swanger, and Richard Vallejo.

Most of all, thank you to you! No book can shine until someone picks it up and reads it.

J.J. and CHRIS GRABENSTEIN are a husband-wife writing team. J.J. is an award-winning voice-over and stage performer, as well as Chris's longtime secret weapon: she reads and edits all his books before anyone else sees them. *Shine!* marks her debut as a coauthor. Chris is the *New York Times* bestselling and award-winning author of many books, including *The Island of Dr. Libris, Escape from Mr. Lemoncello's Library, Mr. Lemoncello's Library Olympics, Mr. Lemoncello's Great Library Race,* and *Mr. Lemoncello's All-Star Breakout Game,* as well as the Welcome to Wonderland series. Chris is also the coauthor of numerous fun and funny page-turners with James Patterson, including *Word of Mouse* and *Max Einstein: The Genius Experiment* and the Jacky Ha-Ha, I Funny, House of Robots, and Treasure Hunters series. J.J. and Chris live in New York City with their cat, Phoebe Squeak, adopted from a local rescue group where J.J. volunteers.

Look for the next Mr. Lemoncello adventure coming in 2020! And visit Chris's website for trailers, bonus quizzes, and more.

ChrisGrabenstein.com